Gathered here today

an open casket of art and poetry

GATHERED HERE TODAY: An Open Casket of Art and Poetry
© 2025 Graveside Press

Published by Graveside Press 2025
graveside-press.com

Editing: Kelley York, Kala Godin
Proofreading: Syd Tomac
Cover illustration: AriBo Art
Cover layout: Sleepy Fox Studio – sleepyfoxstudio.net
Interior Formatting: Sleepy Fox Studio – sleepyfoxstudio.net
Interior Illustrations: AriBo Art

eBook 978-1-967547-97-5
Paperback (KDP) 978-1-967547-94-4
Paperback (Trade) 978-1-967547-95-1
Hardcover 978-1-967547-96-8

No part of this book has been created using Generative AI. Graveside Press and its authors do not consent for our works to be utilized in any form of training for machine learning.

I Am a Human Nesting Doll © 2025 Ian Bain
I Am Haunted © 2025 JJ Carpenter
I think I saw you © 2025 Sam Muller
I'm sorry, my dear © 2025 Rich McFarlin
Idi Amin's Brain © 2025 J. J. Munro
If © 2025 Kelli Dianne Rule
In the Distance Dark (Gargoyle Poem #1) © 2025 Bernardo Villela
In The Stillness © 2025 Foong
Invulation © 2025 Stephen Mcquiggan
Is Something Wrong © 2025 Em Arata-Berkel
Jaded Lament © 2025 Kyle Nowak
Laughter After Dark © 2025 J. E. Norwood
Layered House © 2025 Callum Wilson
Leashed © 2025 Blayne Waterloo
Literal © 2025 Hailey Samford
Man © 2025 Steve Denehan
Masters of Horror © 2025 Hannah Rebekah Graves
Meat in the Machine © 2025 Yelena Crane
Meet the Monsters © 2025 Edward Lodi
Mirielle © 2025 Dee Allen
My Dungeon Ghost © 2025 LindaAnn LoSchiavo
My Father Dies a Second Time © 2025 Jonathan Ukah
Necropoliti © 2025 Gary Every
Nevermore © 2025 AriBo
Nightmare © 2025 Kevin Anderson
Nightmare Narcosis © 2025 Brandon Case
Occasion © 2025 Matt Dennison
Oh, toes © 2025 Phillip E. Dixon
Paradox © 2025 L.G. Testa
Parasite © 2025 Alex Fine
Pep Talk © 2025 Lauren Swiderski
Peter Pumpkin Eater's Most Delectable Carving © 2025 Katherine Quevedo
Playing Fetch with the Demon Boar © 2025 Christopher Collingwood
Please Give Me Scissors © 2025 Krys S Achrem
Poor Little Fellow © 2025 Lee Clark Zumpe
Post-Op © 2025 Megan Cartwright
Rain, Rain, Go Away... © 2025 Ian Klink
Reflection © 2025 Julius
See Here © 2025 Corinne Pollard
Shuck © 2025 Odin Meadows

Cover illustration and interior black + red illustrations (p. 9, 19, 32, 88, 159, 164, 225) by AriBo

p. 15, 31, 59, 196-197, 200-201 licensed from DepositPhotos.com and VectorStock.com.

p. 11 "The Winter of Our Discontent" by Claudia Tong
p. 20 "Parasite" by Alex Fine
p. 22 "The Man and the Skull" by Vincenzo Cohen
p. 26-27 "Smash It" by Kelley York
p. 28 "Devious Dining" by Natalia Díaz Jiménez
p. 35 "Among the Dead" by Tinamarie Cox
p. 43 "Regret" by Kelley York
p. 44-45 "Once Upon a Haunted Dream" by Kelley York
p. 50-51 "Eyes in the Dark" by Kelley York
p. 53 "Date Night" by Camellia Paul
p. 63 "Playing Fetch with the Demon Boar" by Christopher Collingwood
p. 70 "Bones Beneath" by Miranda Allen
p. 78 "The Abyss" by Caterina Minezzi
p. 82-83 "Men in the Room" by Kelley York
p. 84-85 "Bleeding Out in Space" by Kelley York
p. 90 "Nevermore" by AriBo
p. 100-101 "Storm Light" by Drew Golden
p. 107 "Apocalyptic Sun" by Dan Verkys
p. 110 "Please Give Me Scissors" by Krys S Achrem
p. 116-117 "Silence" by Red Wallflower
p. 119 "Reflection" by Julius
p. 123 "Step into the Light" by Kelley York
p. 128-129 "Cabin Fever" by Delana Luna
p. 137 "Homage" by Henna Oak
p. 139 "Guard Your Heart" by Nick Dunkenstein
p. 140-141 "Layered House 1" by Callum Wilson
p. 142 "The Seer" by Terry Campbell

Daniel Gene Barlekamp

There's a Coffin in My Parlor!

There's a coffin in my parlor that's
been here since yesterday.
Some guys in suits just dropped it off
and then they went away.

Don't get me wrong, I must admit
it's really quite a sight,
a shiny mass of oak and brass
reflecting candlelight.

Although this coffin's very nice
there's one small hangup here:
The living never bother me,
for it's the dead I fear.

They're still and cold and awfully old
with eyes that cannot see,
and yet it always seems as though
they're watching you and me.

How I will make it through the night
I truly do not know.
This coffin's in my house and I've
got nowhere else to go.

Who can I call, what can I do,
except just sit and wait?
I've got no phone or Internet,
it's 1858!

I hesitate to think about
what lies inside the box.
If that lid starts to open, I
will jump out of my socks.

What's that I hear? A sound so near
it chills me to the bone.
From deep within the coffin's depths
there comes a gagging groan.

How can this be? It's widely known
cadavers cannot choke.
Instead I tell myself that this
must be some kind of joke.

But now I fear my ears detect
a rustle and a scratch
as something tears the silk inside
to reach the casket's latch.

"Indeed, a joke!" I cry aloud,
my hair now white with fright,
and spring toward that beastly box
to end my ghastly plight.

I start to lift the heavy lid
to see who's got my goat,
when two dead hands reach out and wrap
themselves around my thr—

LL Garland

The Fiddler

Every year on Halloween
A strange musician waits unseen.
He lingers in the old graveyard
With tombs and statues standing guard.

His violin, well-worn with age,
Lodged between arm bones and ribcage.
Yellowed bones clutch an ancient bow
To summon those at rest below.

The tower bell tolls its twelfth peal
As the fiddler begins a reel.
He keeps time on an old tombstone,
Taps the rhythm with his heel bone.

Corpses crawl up through muck and mire
Delighted for what will transpire.
Eagerly the dead heed his call
To dance at the All Hallows' Ball.

Anxious for the dance to begin
They dust their bones, peel rotting skin,
Straighten and clean threadbare grave-clothes.
Just one night, then back to repose.

For fresh partners, the corpses wait
Within the cemetery's gate.
The fiddler's song, on arcane winds,
Speeds through the town and then descends,

Calling to the mortal dancers,
Each wicked soul hears and answers.
Enchanted by his violin,
Dreaming mortals are drawn within.

The long-dead and the freshly so
Choose their partner and off they go.
Clattering bones clutch spectral palm,
Pairing off for this ghastly prom.

The dead assist them through the gloom,
Lead past empty crypt, grave, and tomb.
Each soul in a daze and content
To heed the soloist's lament.

The musician strikes up a waltz.
Dancers whirl over vacant vaults.
Ev'ry couple spins, twirls, and weaves
Between the headstones and yew trees.

And so it goes, all through the night,
They dance, much to the dead's delight.
But festivities grow morose.
They know daybreak is growing close.

Dawn alights with cock's shrieking crow.
The fiddler's gone to rest below.
A portion of each dancer's soul
He takes with him—the player's toll.

Ignorant, the living waken,
Never missing what was taken,
Blissfully they cannot recall
The cold grave that awaits them all.

At work and at home that next day
The dancers hum the fiddler's lay.
Despite fatigue and feet that throb
None remembers the Danse Macabre.

One year hence, the fiddler will rise,
Summon mortals to their demise.
Severed souls are reunited
To dance again with the blighted.

But at first light, with dawn's reprieve
Those souls are not allowed to leave.
For if you've danced to his song twice
A grave is the eternal price.

Alex Carrigan

𝔚𝔦𝔠𝔨𝔢𝔡 𝔖𝔱𝔢𝔭𝔪𝔬𝔱𝔥𝔢𝔯

(A Golden Shovel After Brennan Lee Mulligan)

Your eyes always burn whenever you see **the face**

of the woman sitting quietly in the corner **of a**

darkened guest room. The shadows of her **divinity**

reach into you through your eyelids, so she suggests **you don't**

try to look away. Even from the corner, you feel compelled to **worship**

her, and compelled to placate her growing wrath before she enters **the**

range of candlelight. You have probably realized that you are **fucking**

dead once you can make out the sharpened tips of that insatiable **smile**

of hers, that she will make you one more fool right out **of a**

cautionary tale told to children who think they can escape the **devil.**

You can try to close your eyes again in the vain hope **that you**

can see something brighter than her at the end, but you'll **never**

forget how the stories of fools were the only scripture you **believed in.**

Hannah Rebekah Graves

Masters of Horrors

She was a lot
All right
All dark-haired
And dark-eyed

A witch
Your standard story
Your feeble excuses
Marks that never existed

Cursed and wretched
And destined for so much bloodshed
She conspired with demons
No, worse still
She conspired with her own

She was an evil thing
Her body bore taint
She could bewitch even a king
A martyr
A mistake that no one had actually asked her
    part in

They took her body
And what remained of her head
Shoved both deep in a chest
No bigger than a child's plaything
No more thought than an impulse

And though she showed contrition whilst she
    still breathed
It could not be helped
The way that her blood
The real mark of her innocence
Drained down into the soil
And then down further still

It was a curse
Not from her
But from the crime that took place
And it spelt disaster
For everyone involved in such a ghoulish
    dance

Damn them
Damn them for their lies
Damn them for their frustrations
Damn them for their impatience
Damn them all, for martyrs they pretend to
    be

And her blood rested
Deep in the earth
As the truth sought its revenge
And what had been holy and just
Became instead a blight
The horror where it belonged

Robin Rose Graves

A Reminder:

You left me with the wolves

Hoping I'd keep them fed

I let them eat my legs

So you could run away

I knew you wouldn't take me with you

I knew you wouldn't look back

Asleep, in your worst dreams

You won't see my face

The wrong name spoken

I gave my blood

Stiffed upper lip and attempted a smile

While teeth gnawed on my bones

It was not out of love

I just wasn't sure how to say no

Vincenzo Cohen

𝕿𝖍𝖊 𝕾𝖐𝖚𝖑𝖑

I am like a breath of wind
I melt in the snow...

It's distressing to see with the eyes of a skull
   covering itself upon the horizon
in landing I heard calling me from labyrinth,
from that ocean of wrecks,
precocious mind of child...
The coast is wet and in the morning I chase
   the traces of something that has passed,
   that
perhaps I will not see...
I wander into the darkness that I don't know
   and it belongs to me.

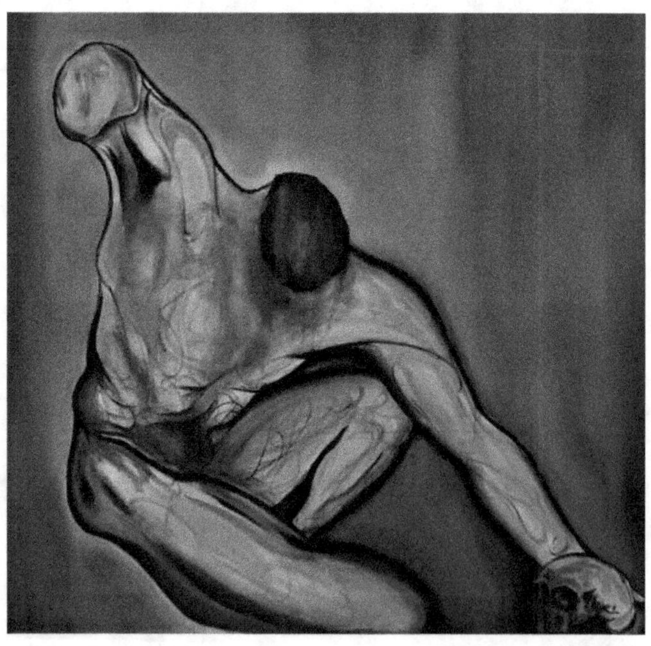

Megan Cartwright

Curios

We rifle through Bluebeard's curios,
knowing killers keep mementos—
a button, a pendant. A severed toe.

Waxen plants quest for moonlight,
their foliage secreting tentacle eyes;
silent cache of gastropod spies.

Like us, they are drawn to disturbance,
to bookcases corseted in cling wrap.
Our hands long to defile paintings,
leave slick silver trails like tearstains—
obliterate faces and landscapes.

Item #12: The preserved cane toad

Articulated skeleton, assembled by drones,
limbs threaded through with picture-wire bones.

Item # 98: The shrine to a shoal

An antique cup filled with shrunken carp;
a pagoda stacked high with shards of pasts.

Item #203: The mannequin-man

A sideshow cowboy in denim and plaid, relic
from when corpses were bought and displayed.

We rifle through Bluebeard's curios.
I spy with my formaldehyde eye,
a finger bone, a peach stone.

Glenis Moore

Fright Night

We always meet on Halloween
when midnight comes around,
when ghosts and demons walk the streets
and vampire wraiths abound.
With trick-or-treaters all in bed
the darkness is our friend.
It gives us space to do our worst
before the season ends.
We curse the goodness in the world,
perform the devil's rites.
It is our job just once a year
to conjure up such frights.
But when the morning sun comes up
you'll find we've gone away,
as though our evil's full of might
it's scared to death of day.

Greg Schwartz

Vessel

dark alley
he hunkers down behind a dumpster
watching the sun disappear

the two holes in his neck
refusing to heal
still oozing fresh blood
through the dirty bandage

he shivers in the cold
sinking low among the garbage
hoping she won't find him
bleed him dry again
discard his wasted body
till it generates more blood
so once again
come nightfall
she can feed.

Rich McFarlin

I'm sorry, my dear

"I'm sorry, my dear, I should have listened to everything you said,"

he said as he swung the hammer and bashed in her big, fat head.

"I should have listened harder, my dear, but I do repeat,"

he said, as he rolled her up inside a stained and darkening sheet.

"I should not have called you fat, my dear, when clearly it was bloat,"

he said as he dragged her body down and flung it into a boat.

"I should have listened close, my dear, and hung on every word,"

he said as he saw the bitch had somewhat slightly kind of stirred.

"I should not have cared so much, my dear, about the pillowcase,"

he said as he swung the hammer and smashed her covered face.

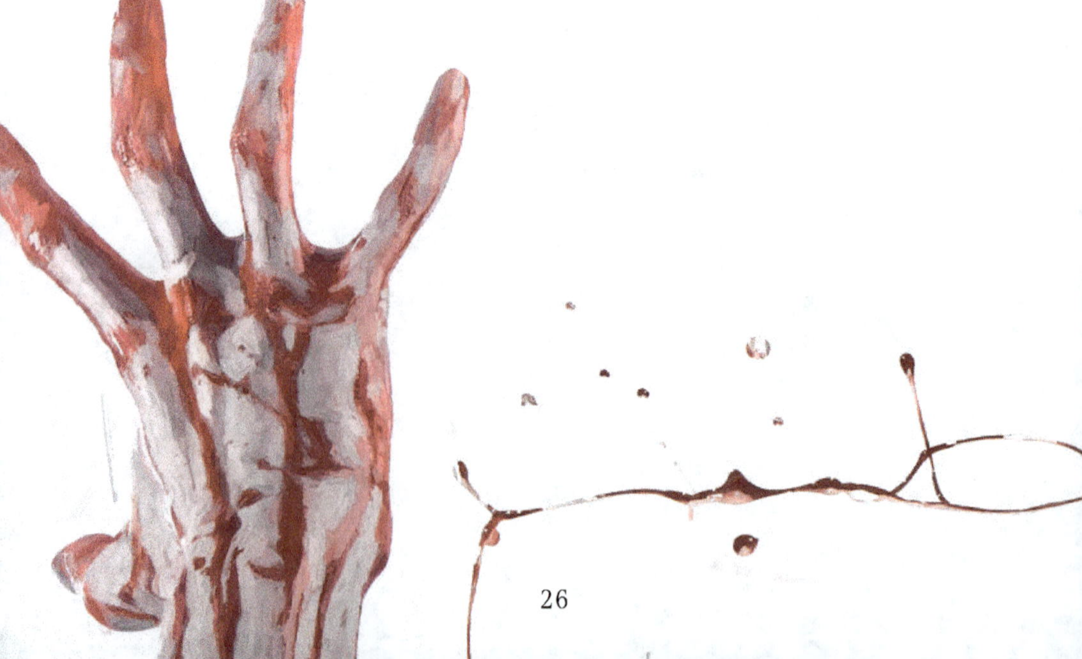

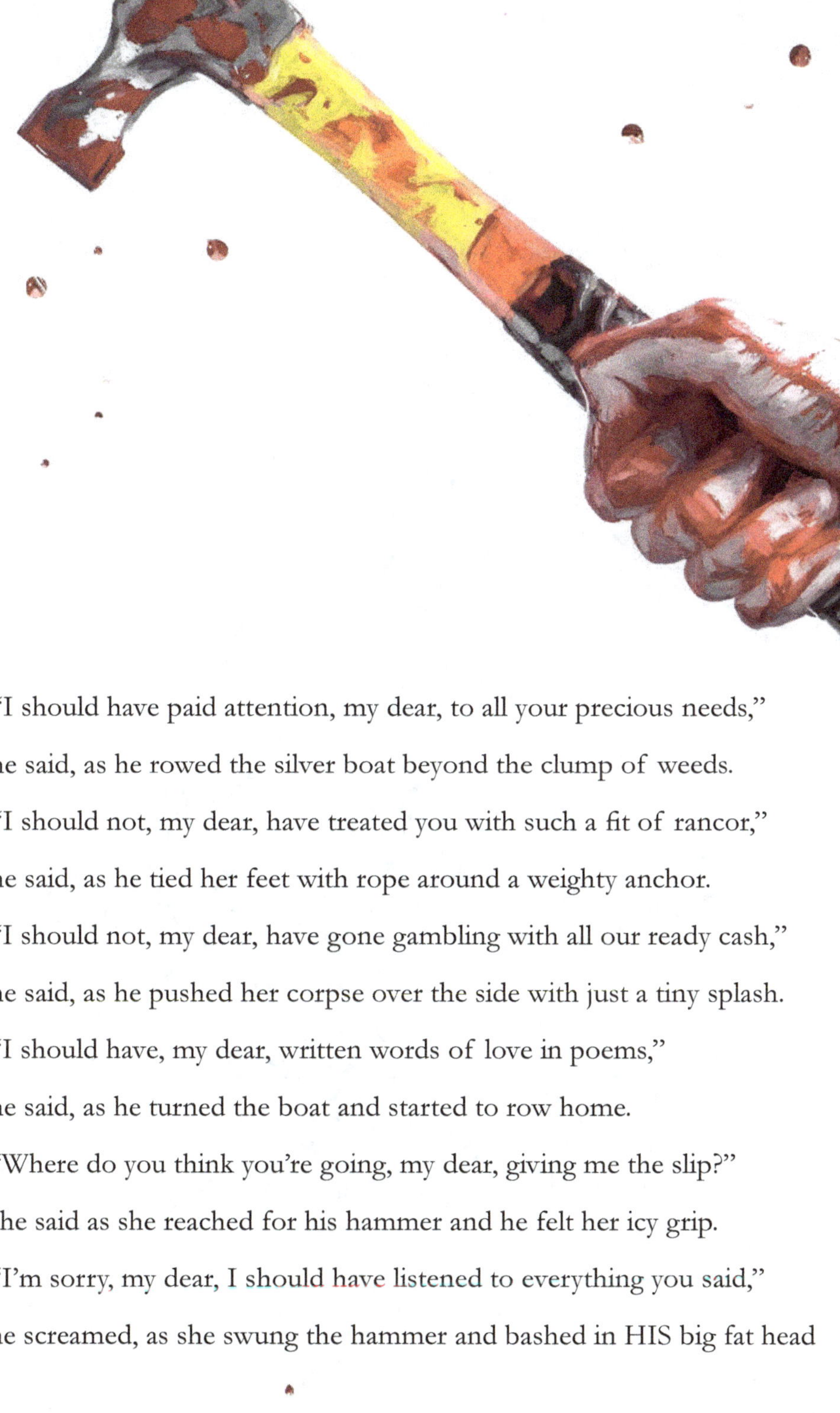

"I should have paid attention, my dear, to all your precious needs,"

he said, as he rowed the silver boat beyond the clump of weeds.

"I should not, my dear, have treated you with such a fit of rancor,"

he said, as he tied her feet with rope around a weighty anchor.

"I should not, my dear, have gone gambling with all our ready cash,"

he said, as he pushed her corpse over the side with just a tiny splash.

"I should have, my dear, written words of love in poems,"

he said, as he turned the boat and started to row home.

"Where do you think you're going, my dear, giving me the slip?"

she said as she reached for his hammer and he felt her icy grip.

"I'm sorry, my dear, I should have listened to everything you said,"

he screamed, as she swung the hammer and bashed in HIS big fat head

Trace McLaurin

Aren't You Hungry?

Aren't you hungry, little child?
You've barely touched your plate.
We've brought you here for supper,
Sans an appetite to sate.

You used to eat like vultures,
Gnawing on fresh carrion.
But your beak won't even open,
But an inch, now, dear. What's wrong?

Would you eat if we had sausage?
Fish or cow? Snail or snake?
Would you choose to eat some mutton,
If I baked it in a cake?

I won't let you go to bed,
Until you've had a bite of meat.
Now choose the flesh that tastes the best,
Or I'll feed you chicken feet!

You haven't had your fill of skin,
Nor bone or blood, nor brain or bladder.
You need to eat a balanced meal,
Before you make me even sadder.

Oh, fine, you little monster.
You don't have to eat this minute.
Your teeth were made for gnashing,
Not this silly little grimace.

I hope you've learned a lesson,
About when dinner gets brought in.
Just know, next time, I'll make you dine,
On the flesh of your own kin.

Gregg Chamberlain

The Zombie Came Back

(based on "The Cat Came Back")

Old Man Johnson had some troubles of his own
There was a hungry zombie would not leave him alone
He tried and he tried to scare the thing away
Even tried to burn it up one hot summer's day.

But the zombie came back the very next day,
The zombie came back, it was here to stay,
The zombie came back, it just wouldn't stay away.

Neighbour next door said he could fix that zombie all right,
Loaded up a pump shotgun with nails and dynamite,
Then he waited and waited for the zombie to come 'round,
Ninety-seven bitty pieces of the neighbour were all that they
found

And that zombie came back the very next day,
Yeah, the zombie came back and was here to stay,
The zombie came back, it just wouldn't stay away.

Old Man Johnson found a hitman for a hundred dollar note,
Told him to take that zombie up the river with a high-speed boat,
So they got a rope around its neck, but it refused to settle down,
And they had to drag the river for the hitman who was drowned.

Then the zombie came back the very next day,
Yep, that zombie was back, and here to stay,
The zombie came back, it just wouldn't stay away.

Now they lured the zombie into a house with a little secret room
Chocked all full of TNT that made a right awful boom,
The whole house came back down in pieces here and there,
With little bits of zombie flesh scattered everywhere.

Still that zombie came back the very next day,
Man, the zombie was back, and it was here to stay,
The zombie came back, 'cause it just wouldn't stay away.

The thunder roared, lighting flashed, and then down came the rain
It wasn't very nice outside as they waited for the train.
The zombie staggered over and began to cross the track
When a westbound freight come along and hit it in the back.

But that zombie came back the very next day
Still the zombie came back, it was here to stay,
Yes, the zombie came back, it just wouldn't stay away.

Well, the nukes came crashing down just the other day,
A-bomb, H-bomb, even a couple neutrons they do say.
So Russia's gone, England's toast, and it was good-night U.S.A.
Yeah, the human race was finished, and without a chance to pray.

But…that dang zombie was back, the very next day,
Yeah, the zombie is back, and it's here to stay,
The zombie came back, it ain't got the brains to stay away.

Kenneth D. Reimer

The Song of the Corpse

Methought as I wandered on a moonlit night,
through graves and tombstones in shadows bedight
mingled with the flutter of a black owl's wing,
I heard a broken and bloodless voice sing.
I stiffened and trembled at so ghastly a sound
then with unseemly haste to the frost-covered ground
dashed my pale, timid body, swept over with fear
by the song of a corpse so dreadfully near.
The voice, how it lilted in each dry, mournful wail
recounting the horrors of its grisly tale,
and though I pressed to the earth and covered my ear
in the still, moon-washed evening, I started to hear…

"It was a cold winter day," said the voice of the dead,
"when they prayed, filled the hole, set the stone over my head.
I could scarce hear their footsteps as they hurried away
muffled as they were by six feet of clay.
Then I lay calm and quiet, with my solitary ideas
'til spring thaw brought the searching of worms to my ears.
I remember my terror when I first realized
that the things they'd like most were the whites of my eyes.
I screamed for assistance but there came no reply.
People forget you after you die.
No one came to visit; there were none buried around,
So out of sheer desperation, I crawled up from the ground.
In the dry summer winds, my flesh turns to dust,
and the brown flakes on my eyelids remind me of rust.
It's better now, though I've sped up the decay,
at least in the daylight, the worms stay away.
I wouldn't exchange it; I won't go back in,
better to fade on my tombstone, than have holes in my skin.
I've nothing to gain, so I wouldn't tell lies.
It's better to burn us when somebody dies."

With that final declaration, he let out a dry moan,
and I bolted upright and scrambled back home.
I haven't returned; I go to the library at nights.
The worms you find there have less grisly appetites.

Stephanie Valente

When We Were Vampires

Strangers turned to stone like fallen kings.
Mortals were too precious. We forgot sunlight.
Your hand lingered on my back. You rubbed
rosemary into my neck. Rites and delights.
In fruit groves and bad men, we took over
entire towns, and we always needed more blood.
We thought as saviors with bits of prophecy,
my body ached every night. Fruit rotted.
Our souls shiny oil-black, ready to pounce.
Like bridal nuns in criminality, chewing parsley,
I straddled you until those lips grew purple.
Teeth freshly sharpened. Neck bitten.
We melted. Entranced, in dreams where
you always loved me. We gnawed
on the city's soul without apology.

Kurt Newton

A Cold, Windswept Place

My soul is a cold, windswept place,
My heart a barren womb.
My life a man without a face,
My spirit embalmed, entombed.

How this misfortune came to be,
The events are cloudy still,
A wide-eyed boy, once pure and sweet,
Who forfeited free will.

She was all I ever dreamed and more,
Her face, her hair, her touch…
She knew me like no other before,
And I loved her, oh, so much.

But seduction is a feral beast,
With fathomless eyes and supple lips.
Once attached, she began to feast,
Slowly, drip by drip.

I knew not such creatures existed then,
Such vile, beguiling things,
That exploit the weaknesses of men,
And the self-loathing that it brings.

For years, she came to me at night,
In a foggy, love-sick haze,
Slipping in and out of sight,
Until my final days.

She left me upon our eternal bed,
In a pool of betrayal and musk.
The man upon which she once fed,
Was now a hollow, sorrowful husk.

Now, I have no choice but to be one of them,
A creature more dead than alive,
Whose rosy mouth belies a thorny stem,
And an undying thirst to survive.

Todd Matson

The Feeder

Why? you ask.
Do you really need
me to answer? Just look
around. Behold the multitude
of bird feeders in her yard, the sugar
dispensers for the hummingbirds, the salt
licks for the deer, the open trashcan full of leftovers
for the racoons, the squirrel feeders in her trees, the bread
crumbs around her pond for the geese, the nuts and grains scattered
about for the chipmunks, the garden of leafy greens for the
rabbits. Do you still not understand? Because she could
never bring herself to discriminate. She loved all
of God's creatures, including the vampire
living in her basement. What else
could she do? A creature can't
help but to be what it is.
You called her an
enabler, an accomplice
to her child's self-destruction.
She told you she only wanted to be
like Jesus who gave his blood for us so
that we could live. You told her she was in denial.
She claimed you were heartless. What loving parent, after
all, would not take out home equity loans, max out their credit cards,
drain their retirement accounts to bail out their child, pay their
bond, legal fees and court costs, declare bankruptcy,
foreclose on their homes and fork over their
social security checks to save their
child? You told her that her
son was an addict. She
explained how everyone has
their problems. And she did it. She
allowed him to drain her of her last ounce
of blood until she was sprawled out on the floor,
pale and lifeless, the modern-day Jesus of her dreams.
Spread the news. Tell your neighbors. Prepare
your feeders. Very soon you will be
visited by myriad insatiable
woodland creatures
and a vampire.

Katherine Garrison

Castle Reflections

It rose from the depths—
perhaps even from the core of the earth.
Oxidized red iron dirt surging from below as it grew.
Molten, turning ash white. Pale stone not of *here*. Ethereal.

Those who stumble across it claim it has sat for millennia,
and I would agree, but that I'd seen its birth.
More likely, I think, it sat beneath the earth's crust,
waiting and rotting for eons before emerging.

In the night, people claim to hear its ghosts.
A projection of the fanciful objects of their imaginations.
An attempt to pin its existence down.
To smother their fears.

The *clip-clops* of those returned from medieval war.
Swords ringing in the courtyard.
Wails of loved ones at execution spectacles.
The peal of bells and recitation of psalms in the dark.
Barks of laughter, revelling souls and crackling fires.

They claim the smells of roasting meats and hot fat still waft.
Soaked into the stonework, a stain.
I know they haven't gotten close enough to confirm this.

For if they did, they would smell a putrid stench.
Sulphurous gas seeping from its almost impenetrable guts.
Once, I found a way in—
through a fetid wound open at its base.
Tucked behind weaving ivy, beckoning me.
I gagged, clawing through its sharpness
and reaching a vaulted chamber;
my own breath echoed back at me.
The feeling of one million pins needling my skin.

Rough-hewn platforms of dark stone jutted from the walls,
on top of which lay versions of a self I never had—never would become.
Dozens of accusing, milky eyes choked me as I clambered away.

No, this is not one of those fairytale castles.
I shudder as the death stares of my *could-have-beens,*
swim in my periphery at its every mention.
It is a mirror—one that reflects answers to
questions better left unknown.

J. E. Norwood

Laughter After Dark

In the dead of night, their laughter haunts me,
as their human shapes grow less familiar
In alleys, bars and gutters, the day burns at the stake
and profanities possessing throats and tongues proliferate

Excised like sickness, I know not my fellow man,
forced to lurk and always look about
I spy them sharpening daggers 'round every corner,
now those kindly smiles reveal their dreadful truths

The thing by day, a harbinger of peace,
by night becomes a different beast
A reminder of their sheer totality,
and that there is no safety to be had

I live in shadow yet I cannot hide,
invariably discovered by those prowling eyes
And as they peel back their ruddy lips,
there is no love in their laughter

In a dream, I laughed along,
but I seem to have forgotten how
As the light is squeezed through the gullet of night,
I am swallowed by their laughter

Phinn Disario

What Echoes are Left

I have a ghost that follows me around
A sinister laugh for a tenuous crown
I thought I had left this darkness behind
The harrowing night my grandmother died

But a spectral hand tightened around my throat
And all the blood paintings were starting to float
I couldn't breathe and I couldn't think
The world around me began to shrink

The crown is slipping off my head
If it all comes down, I will surely be dead
I held her dear portrait gripped in my hand
This pain is a phantom I now understand

Ritiksha Sharma

Specimen 401 (a)

I

At first, Hector was born
With extracurricular stimuli, having been had
Like a dinner table fool, consuming
an intellectual protest

I Wrote
> *Specimen 401 (a) woke up disoriented.*

A chained gorgon, gorged,
then disemboweled
Charmed by the mere whiff, a life of agency
and intelligence, circling his fingertips

And my hands trembling,
Curiosity outpaced by concern
Was newfound and arresting
Audaciously, wondered
> *How does it feel to be you?*

Out rose a matter of logistics
His motionless frame and my imagination stirred

So, I reassigned Specimen 401 (a) an identity,
his very first, his very own,
my creatured-chum

Had to be perfunctory
The stitches on his face
Had to be ubiquitous; his empty eyes
filled with the glory of my invention;
Had to follow the scientific,
not the psychological.

II

Then Hector was unhinged
Looking from his side of the lab
Sat glaring, smiles and teeth blaring
Wrote on the wall

*Mother, tell me,
do you want to build a man?*

Teleported on my lap
Whispered

Do you know what your eyes look like?

Watched me shaking my head
Like a silent death-siren; stuck out
the tip of his nail against my cheek

Then I will paint, then liquid red.

Broke skin with a prick; I wailed, he smiled

The logical fear I manufactured,
from a condition purely biological
Ran out on me

So, I offered him, redundant replicas of emotion

*He could be momentarily enthralled;
maybe I would write about his mortality,
if he would leave mine alone*

Mined out of deterrence-determination, sudden
yearning for life; festered in the cornea,
beside a creator's dilemma, my conscience
had failed seconds prior

I scrambled for words, inaudibility, breaking out with

Hec….cc…tor?

His image, the faces in his face,
the concurrency of his stitches

Looked back into his dead eyes,
a petrified image formed upside down, a face,
my very own, was drowning in the glacial dark.
I cried red from the now-empty sinkholes. Looked
into the lines, following the blackness
jettisoned; synthesised perennially
The wormhole overextended
between us
Closed my eyes and whimpered,
Maybe I can calm him down

Are you okay? How are you feeling?

He pushed his nail past my iris

You are about to find out.

Dug out my eyeballs, scarred soft skin; and I made
one last mental note, a final inquiry quenched

Frankenstein's science was all about
the intangible psychological,
and,

*Specimen 401 (a) had been in pain
all alone, all along.*

Brandon Case

𝕹ightmare 𝕹arcosis

Black water, staccato heartbeat, kilometers of flooded stone
shadows compress my headlamp
my respirator hisses
Khhh-cck.

Neoprene gloves, pink guide rope, my partner descends
into the dark crevasse
through a crack
I remove my air tank, shove it ahead
rocks scrape yellow paint
my chest too wide, I'm stuck
a hard exhale
I squeeze through
into the Devil's Chamber
most scuba deaths of any cave
skulls and crossbones mark our path
we continue
Khhh-cck.

My partner turns
double thumbs-up for the camera
he doesn't see the shadows rise
behind him
a grabbing darkness
clouds of silt, thrashing
a gurgled scream
fades to breathless silence.

When the water clears, I'm alone
my pink guide rope is gone
directionless black, forever
tight against my skin
my regulator flashes red
Cck-cck.

Katherine Kerestman

Bobby's Adventure

Bobby saw a great big black cat
Run past his house and sail around
The corner in ten seconds flat.
The boy's feet barely touched the ground,

So quick he was in his pursuit
Of the charcoal cat that he failed
To note the concealed plunging chute,
(Plunged into somber gloom, he wailed)

Hidden beneath flattened boxes,
To catch wayward children when they roam,
Drop them in dank realms, obnoxious,
Who shall nevermore go back home.

Bobby squinted in the blackness,
Rubbed his eyes and looked about him,
His young heart heavy with sadness,
His eyes searched the prison grim.

Instead, heard the accursed beasts,
Heard the hideous monsters roar.
Heard the eldritch goat-gods' bleats,
And bubbling of foul fish-men four.

Overheard their conversation.
"Ph'nglui mglw'nafh Cthulhu R'lyeh wgah'nagl fhtagn,"
They croaked and coughed their incantation,
Invoked The Sleeping One again.

Bristly, dark pink, star-shaped creatures,
Fungoid dwellers in mildewed tombs,
Winged reptiles with piscine features,
Shriek in black and formless gloom,

"Ph'nglui mglw'nafh Cthulhu R'lyeh wgah'nagl fhtagn."
Bobby had no dictionary,
Nor needed one to understand;
The primal nature in him, wary.

He felt his way through lightless halls,
Tread cautiously the slippery floor,
Saw a red glow through the rock walls;
He hoped it was an egress door.

Step by step, he made his dark way,
To the red glow in the distance,
Afraid to stray, fearful to stay,
Relied on instinct in this instance.

As he drew near, the red glow formed,
A rectangle-shape, as of a door,
Only it was twisted, malformed—
From beyond it came a clamor,

Door burst open! From it upsurged,
Phantasmagoric spectrous ghouls.
Beyond, needled spires (submerged),
Minarets, domes 'neath crimson pools.

Foamy red waves, bilious red surf,
Stretched out to the red horizon,
Three red moons span the entire girth,
Blood-red sky for fiends to rise in.

Cursed doorway, unclean portal
To loathsome grotto, carmine shore.
Furry thing brushed Bobby's ankle—
Big black cat that he'd chased before.

Cat mewed and rubbed his soiled shoe,
And Bobby knew he wanted to,
Guide him from out the nameless slough—
But what good could a feline do?

In the dark void, cat's eyes glistened,
The great black cat tugged Bobby's pants,
Put his ear on wall and listened,
To heathen, weird, blasphemous rants,

Emanating from the tunnels.
Big black cat slunk in the shadows,
Bobby following at his heels,
Slinking past the forms unhallowed.

Crawling over crumbled stone walls,
They squeezed through chinks in mouldy floors,
Descended to a hexagonal,
Room with blood-soaked earthen floor.

The big black cat signaled the boy
To raise the iron covering.
Requiring Bobby to employ
All his strength, his muscles quivering.

Cat leapt into the darkened vault,
Meowed for Bobby to follow.
From behind, a roisterous tumult—
Slurps and curses, hisses, growls—

Bobby jumped into the hole.
What a wonder! Blue and green,
Pink and yellow rainbow below,
Most brilliant thing he'd ever seen.

Hordes of soft and furred beasties,
Cats of every shape—all sizes,
Hied from all the earthly countries,
Some from light-years beyond the skies,

Come together in the Cat Land,
A weird dimension all its own,
A place where humans seldom stand.
The kits and cats and sires have known,

For it was (long ago) foretold,
That a boy would come to live there,
Play with young kittens, cuddle the old
Make his bed with them fore'er.

The big black cat looks in his eyes,
Bobby knows they want him to stay,
But, wishing to go home, he tries,
To ask their help to get away,

Away from Cat Land's rainbow-hues,
Away from subterranean red,
Roiling waters, from ghastly crews,
From mildewy tombs, creatures dread.

Back to his mom and dad and bed,
Back to his school and baseball bat—
The big black cat, he shakes his head,
The boy must stay where he is at.

It is a pleasant place withal,
The kits, they need a pet to love,
To feed and clean, cuddle and call,
"Bobby, boy, oh, come here dove,

Here, Bobby, Bobby, here, boy, boy,"
To pull the string and roll the ball,
A boy to call their own sweet toy.
Bobby says, "thanks, black cat, but no."

He wants to go back to his home.
There's no way back, he must realize,
Beloved pet in rainbow zone,
Else hors d'ouevres, grisly human fries.

(Voracious hybrid reptile gods,
Are 'specially fond of human meat!)
Bobby ends his days in paws,
Pulling strings and offering treats,

A mad old man whose nine foot beard,
Twelve kittens race to climb up on,
A mad old man who speaks in weird,
Meows. To Fate he wast a pawn.

JB Wocoski

When the Black Cat Mews

On the longest, darkest night of the year
with the wind howling, giving you fear,
appeared an apparition, of a black cat
outside your window, on the sill it sat.
Biding its time, it never mews.

Not ever mewing even once to be let in.
Not scratching, not fussing, not making a din.
Instead, sitting out there, it just stared
through the panes of glass, its eyes glared.
Biding its time, it never mews.

You rub your eyes in total disbelief
that a cat sat waiting to be debriefed,
or was it waiting for you to confess
something evil that you did? Truly, I jest.
Biding its time, it never mews.

Why does it sit there and stare at you?
Why not leave? It could elsewhere be
some place, warm, rolled into a ball.
Some place else, like in a funeral hall.
No longer biding its time, it mews.

It no longer sits on the windowsill.
I do believe you're going to hell.
Somehow, it's sitting inside your room.
Why do you get that sense of doom?
It's now past your time, obituary news.

Jim. G. Burns

snapshots from the hole

white is black

in the hole

noise is silence

cat purrs

hum through

hypnagogic haze

silly boy

and long-gone girl

tussle in tall grass

bear cubs released

from winter's den

lips are kissed

then silenced

tears float and fall

petals from bouquets

thrown at weddings

but the hole

will not release

its dead

Jayde Fontana

The Prying Eye

Many gaze at the sky's pale eye
But few know it gazes back
Well I saw, at the grave where my brother lies
When its pale light broke the empty black
Of the never-ending skies

I stood beside his wife
I embraced her and we wept
We mourned the loss of a life
That was claimed while we had slept

I held her with tender love and care
But when I looked up from her brown hair
I was shocked at what was there

I beheld a woman and man
Huddled by the gate
They watched us and I knew not their plan
My grief transformed to hate

"Leave us be!" I shouted
"Let us mourn in peace!"
The watchers left, my vision clouded
With tears that would not cease

But another watcher stood in the sky
Violating the safety of our cry
Though she didn't notice the evil eye

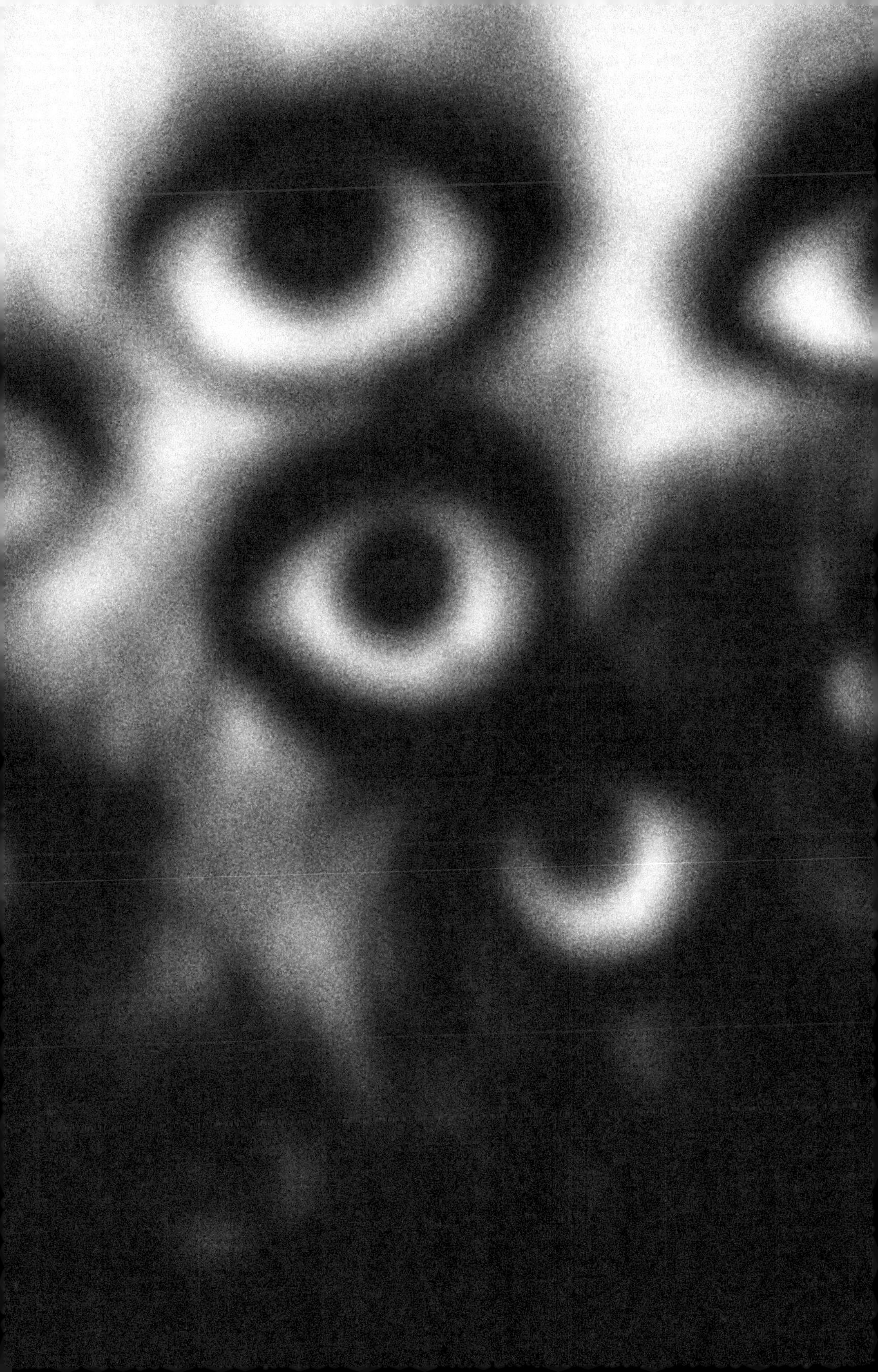

It shined down and exposed our grief
All could see our pouring tears
No privacy to find relief
I looked upon the thing with fear

"Come," I said to her, "we should leave this ghastly place."
I took her hand and led her home at a swiftly pace
But she did not see the fear that lay upon my face

All that night while she stayed asleep
Oblivious to the stare from above
Through the windows its light would creep
Mocking us for our lost love

I had to save her from its stare
For she suffered just as I
At least her brother had been spared
Shielded from the eye

At that thought I finally knew
Just what I needed…had to do
To save us from the horrid hue

The monster's gaze would never cease
So I had to shield her from its prying
I raised her body to find her peace
From the sky's vicious spying

I walked to the cellar and laid her on the floor
Where we'd be safe to mourn alone
But she woke as I reached the door
"Whatever are you doing?" she said with a moan

"Here, it cannot see us. I will not let it in!"
I explained as I chained the door shut with a grin
"The darkness will shield us, if we let it take us in."

She cried, "I am deathly scared."
I responded, "Yes, that's why we're here!
Here that monstrous thing can't stare!"
She ran for the door and I twitched with fear

"You make no sense!" she shrieked
"Let me out right now!"
Tears fell down upon her cheek
As she grabbed the door, I felt sweat on my brow

I said, "We cannot leave! It will never let us be!"
I would not let that monster continue to torment her or me
I picked up a nearby bottle when she ignored my plea

Then there was a crash, and a rain of glass and red
Trickling down her face, from the crown of her head

And now here we are, and here we will forever stay
Safe, like my brother, from the pale eye's staring ray

Evan Baughfman

𝕴 𝕾𝖕𝖔𝖔𝖐𝖞 𝕳𝖆𝖎𝖐𝖚𝖘

Skies azure, breeze light
Leaves rustling, sunshine smiles wide
Dracula's bad day

-

Honey! You…You're here…
"Happy Anniversary"?!
You…died. Remember?

-

Craft beer blind taste test
Wolfsbane-infused IPA
Lycanthrope spits, screams

Ian Klink

Rain, rain, go away

I look inside the closet door
Knowing the beast is there for more
Rain, rain, go away
I pray you don't take me today

It had been there for a long, long time
Dining on this fear and fright of mine
Had it arrived before we were there
Another young child afraid of its stare

Knowing I am no different from any of you
I fear the night as most children do
Though I am no angel in how I behave
I pray I will be spared from fear this way

Should it be so scary of fright
Hovering in and out of the light
It floats inside, awaiting my fall
I wish it would never come at all

My parents will protect me, I think
From all the evils inside that stink
To experience such fear, such horrid sights
Give me the strength to triumph with might

Though I wish I knew its meaning
I fear my bravery weaning
To look in and see the fright
Hovering there all through the night

To ask for a life free of worry
It is too much to ask, surely
But nothing I know can ever compare
To how the horror lurks and stares

I sage my room and sprinkle the salt
Hoping and praying it will halt
My mind says this will help for sure
Yet there it is each night with lure

What are you and why do you come
To my closet instead of some
A monster is nothing but a lost soul
Who forgot to pay the ultimate toll

Try as I might, and try as I may
To get away from this every day
But I see its eyes and see the smile
Fogging up my window for a while

The eyes seek for darkness of man
Trying to get to me as best it can
Oh rain, rain, go away
Your thunderous noises do dismay

Why such hatred and fury inside
As if the hatred will never tide
A dream is like a life awake
But my eyes know it is not fake

To let the beast claim to zero
To summon up the courage of heroes
With a baseball bat in my tiny hands
I look at the closet to take my stand

My feet shuffle, my body abound
Aware of every creak, moan, and sound
The grip in my hands covered in sweat
Soon to have all these memories to forget

Will it scare me with its claws and teeth
A hideous body with green blood beneath
Its eyes are scary and beady and mean
Its wits surely sharper than mine and lean

I reach for the door with a hand that shakes
Again, praying away those who forsake
Shall I be brave or should I be frightened
As the monster lurks, my fear is heightened

The door flies open and I swing quite manic
Though my blood pulsates with panic
I wish to see with my own two eyes
A thing I hope with every strike will die

I finally open my eyes to the fear
Oh my, oh my, my dear
There is absolutely nothing there
Except the clothes and toys broken everywhere

I wipe my brow, rush back to my bed
Laying down my sweaty head
Only to look out the windowsill
To see the beady eyes looking to kill

Oh rain, oh rain. Please. Please, go away.

Azure Arther

A Gorgon at the End of the World

So, she struck out, no destination in mind, because destinations
    no longer mattered.
Every direction was death,
    if you were lucky,
    or weak,
    or useful,
    or any of the things no one wants to be when anarchy rules.
She still put a flower in her hair though,
    plastic with dirty petals pierced
    with the new horns that grew when the civilized world died.
They were hard as bone, these horns,
    unable to be cut by a knife, and the curled ridges,
    once signifiers of the end, were now reminders.
Not just for her, but for all the former humans, now monsters, left.
With horns, like hers,
    or fur, like her neighbors,
    or scales, which she also had,
    or hooves, that chased people down,
    or extra rows of teeth, often whispered about.

All mementos from when the birds stopped,
    some in mid-flight,
    and the thumps of bodies were heard for days,
    not just the birds, but people,
    randomly, casually, without permission,
    dying and dropping where they stood.
She still had her feet though,
    which meant she could still fit her favorite shoes,
    bought when money counted, when capitalism ruled.
It didn't matter that the laces sliced scales from her fingers,
    that she was clumsy with the ties.
Her blood was poison.
To come near her was death.
She shouldered her bag,
    left the remnants of her home,
    and relished in the safety of being a woman,
    walking alone.

Greg Beatty

𝔚𝔥𝔢𝔫 ℑ 𝔇𝔦𝔢, ℑ 𝔚𝔦𝔩𝔩 𝔚𝔞𝔩𝔨

When I die, I will walk

my dog as I do now:

my incorporeal heart drifting

at the end of his leash

as his does on mine now.

Julia LaFond

𝔚𝔬𝔩𝔳𝔢𝔰

Don't stray from the path
That winds through the dark forest:
The wolves are howling.

Don't talk to strangers:
They'll grin with wolf-sharp teeth as
They eat you alive.

Don't stop to rest, for
Your red, hooded cloak stands out
Like blood on the snow.

The little girl did
Exactly as she was told:
She arrived safely

Only to find that
The wolf she should have feared was
Her own grandmother.

Thomas Sudell

The Bretwalda

Who with unhallowed feet dares tread my tomb?
I hear thee, stranger, from my bed of years—
thy sundered accents, like mine own yet strange—
the scraping of thy pick; nor thine alone!
For see! My lordly barrow which hath stood
inviolate for seven hundred years
and seven hundred more is now o'errun
with thieves intent on pillage. Robbers all!
Nor think that though mine own be turned to dust
my helm's imperishable eyes are blind.
They saw my firstborn slain amid the clash
of sword on trenchant sword and shed no tear.
The sun they viewed unblinking as it set
behind his burial mound—nay ask not where!
Think'st thou, O ímpious stranger, that such eyes
were ever closed in slumber or in death?
Nay truly, from beneath their gilded brows
like double points of flame they pierce the mould
to fix upon thee, kneeling in the dirt
but inches from where even now I lie
with hand on hilt. And more they see, far more:
thy cynicism and irrev'rent doubt

that men were ever noble, leaders just,
or converts capable of reasoned thought;
thine arrogance, thy pride—all these they see
and last, pre-eminent above its peers,
thy greed—no stranger to a king who met,
opposed, and overcame it in himself
when tempted to betray an exiled prince.
Ye know the tale, ye know it and ye doubt.
And yet 'twas even so. I conquered greed
and set my guest upon his northern throne,
wherefore I now denounce the grasping thief
who claims to covet neither gold nor gems,
desiring only knowledge of the past,
yet takes the treasures, and the wisdom spurns.
Howbeit, I condemn not love of gold
in one who holds his avarice at bay.
Not I who daily wore upon my belt
the weregild of a nobleman; not I
who bade my kinsmen lay me in the earth
with treasures worthy of a barrow-drake.
For fair indeed is gold. But fairer still
the deed that earns it. Be not over-swift
therefore to doubt the honour of the kings
whose graves ye desecrate, for thus ye lose
the better part of that which therein lies:
not wealth, but rather bittersweet regret
that men are not today what once they were.
If gold prefer'st, then truly, all is lost.

Dee Allen.

𝕸𝖎𝖗𝖎𝖊𝖑𝖑𝖊

Nothing gives her more delight
Than to see the seasons shift.
Long days of summer—the warm, the bright—
Give way to the coming brisk wind's drift.

She smiles when leaves fall,
Turn yellow, orange, from luxuriant green.
Dry, brittle shells blanket all
And tree branches blown bare, suddenly clean.

Then bushes follow the trees' lead.
Open field went withered brown.
Wilting process—every flower and weed—
When overcast grey clouds loom 'round.

In her red wool hooded cape, the caramel-coloured lady meets a
     cooler clime,
Walks past standing tombs, faces one with a familiar name, then
Recalls her glory days in Tremé—Antebellum time—
When her mother threw lavish parties, shown her off to wealthy
     White men.

Dark cholera struck New Orleans and the escaping riverboats.
With the rich on-board, she perished—saw neither Heaven nor
     Hell.
Among us, she returns every Autumn as a wandering ghost.
Lonesome Miss Dupree. First name: Mirielle.

[For Kenna DeValor.]

Sam Muller

I think I saw you

I think I saw you
Last night,
Walking down the river path.

You were carrying the umbrella I got you
For your last birthday,
The one with dragonflies. And I wondered,
Why carry an umbrella in the night? Why?
When the sky is clear, and the only thing raining is starlight.

Perhaps I didn't see you.
Perhaps it was someone like you.
Why should I trust the evidence of my own eyes? Or even my
  ears?

Last week, I thought I saw a dragon,
With gleaming bronze scales and translucent wings,
A dragon wearing a gold choker and carrying an old-fashioned
  lorgnette,
Sitting on the meadow by the river.
He, or perhaps it was she,
Regarded me through the glass, not with hostility but with interest.
The same way I look at specimens through the microscope.
He, or perhaps it was she,
Greeted me in a nasal voice,
And in grammatically flawless English.

So why should I trust my eyes?
Or even my ears?
When I see dragons
And hear them talking to me.

It couldn't have been you I saw.
How can I see you? It is not possible,
I was the first one to throw in a handful of soil,
Black and moist; it had rained the night before.

But perhaps it was you.
Perhaps I did see a dragon in a choker and heard him—or her—
    greet me,
In a nasal voice, and in grammatically flawless English.
Perhaps when I went up to the attic two nights ago,
To look for something,
I've forgotten what,
I actually stepped into a glade bisected by a stream,
And ringed by trees.
The kind of place you encounter in a dream,
Except that I was not dreaming.
I pinched myself, but didn't wake up.
I felt the wind in my face, and the long grass brushing against my
    legs.
When I knelt by the stream and put my hand in,
The water rippled over my fingers,
Carrying with them a hint of snow.

Perhaps seeing you was like going into the attic and finding a
    pastoral scene,
A scene out of a picture I remember from somewhere.
An art gallery, a magazine, a childhood book of fairytales,
Perhaps what I saw was not you,
But my memory of you.

Then where is the umbrella?
The umbrella with dragonflies,
My last birthday present
To you?
What happened to that umbrella?
I looked for it in all the likely places,
And unlikely places, too.
I took a day off,
They were very nice about it at the school.
Of course I didn't tell them why.
If I had,
They wouldn't have laughed at me or told me I was mad.
They would have asked me to sit down,
Given me tea, and biscuits,
Told me to take a holiday, two weeks, even a month.
And the moment I left,
They would have called someone in the family
And said get help.
Fast. Now. Before it is too late.

Is the umbrella with you?
Did I really see you carrying the umbrella with dragonflies,
    heading towards your new home?
The patch of lawn by the river,
Surrounded by frangipani trees.

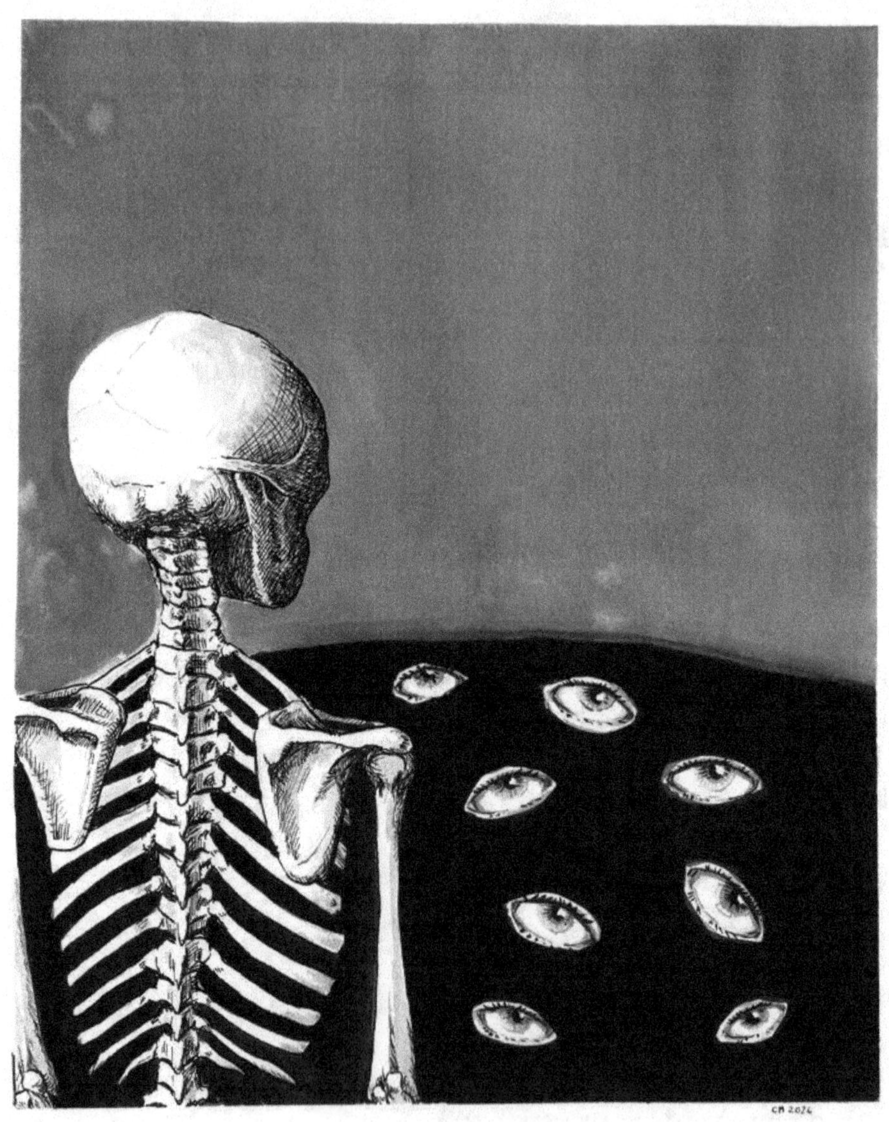

This morning, I didn't see your tote,
The red leather one,
In its usual place on your work desk,
Right next to your laptop,
Where I had placed it,
The day I returned home,
After identifying you,
After drinking the tea they forced on me,
Carrying the bundle of things they gave me.
Personal effects, they called it.

I know no one took the tote.
I saw it when I was looking for the umbrella,
Sitting on your work desk,
Right where I put it,
That night.

So where is the tote?

Tonight I will stand by the gate,
And if I see you again, carrying the umbrella with dragonflies
And the red leather tote,
Then I will know it is you, really you.
Would it then mean that I actually saw a dragon?
And that the door to our attic can sometimes open into another
    world?

Tonight I will stand by the gate,
And if I see you again, carrying the umbrella and the tote,
I will walk behind you,
Down the road, take the turn to the left,
Along the river path,
Until we reach the green patch surrounded by frangipani trees.

Will you then turn around,
Look me in the eye,
Smile
That special smile you kept for me,
And tell me
What this is all about?

But
If you can unravel
The mystery of the dragon,
Would it then mean you also know
The name of the mushrooms I tended with such loving care
In the back garden?
The blood-red ones with butter-yellow spots.
If you can unravel
The mystery of the world behind the attic door
Would it then mean you know,
Where that taste you complained about
In the coffee came from?
The coffee I made for you,
At our last breakfast.

Sarah E Das Gupta

Dark Feasting

(The Day of the Dead)

Today the invisible line
between Man
and that other world
of magic, enchantment, and Death
is crossed by hordes of spirits.
They appear to mortals in
strange guise.
Devils pick belladonna,
hemlock, monk's hood
kept in glass jars of shadowy blue.
Satan's minions,
invisible to human eyes,
feasting on adders' tongues,
stab hearts with knives
sharpened in Wayland's forge.
Skeletal wraiths
haunt new-dug tombs
to feed on grave wax.
In deep woods,
dark spirits
search for deadly mushrooms,
rotting, fleshy fungus
to lay before
drunken sots
on tavern benches.
The putrid dead
search desolate graveyards
for all of Death's detritus.
Phantom vultures
fight over festering
bones.

Tinamarie Cox

Feeding the Shadows

The shadows follow closely,
too close.

(Coming closer.)

I feel their heavy presences all around me,
lurking.

(Stalking.)

My shadows rise up and over me,
obstructing light.

(Posing to strike.)

Coating my world in their darkness,
blinding me.

(Ready to feed.)

And in the endless night that they bring,
I fall onto my knees and ask:
Can prayers come too late?

Lorraine Schein

Ghosts Haunt Space

The Fallen Astronaut Memorial on the moon
honors those fallen American and Soviet travelers:
the ones who never made it up
and those, like us, who died there.

Our bodies bloated, ballooning
like the expanding universe
as our brains lost consciousness,
absorbed into dark matter,
blood vaporized into swirling red gas.

The liquid in our eyes
and tongue boiling away,
as our lungs explode.

When we pass near a sun,
our bodies will dry up from radiation,
becoming skin-blackened,
then frozen space meat.

If you find us, will your crew bring us aboard
to return our remains to our families on Earth
or leave us still following the ship's trajectory?

We will haunt your next astronauts
when they soar by the trail
of our accumulated corpses,
as we drift forever, buried in space's dark loam
with only a bouquet of stars
to mark our shifting gravesite.

Jacqueline K Goldblatt

Before He Stays

   There's vulnerability in remembering.
The blossoming of the eye,
Slackening of hands as the familiar
Ache,
Pulse,
Pull,
Of the past hooks itself into the doorknocker,
Of the heart and bids itself welcome.

This is not a ghost story.
This never was a ghost story.
And yet…

What is memory but a continual haunting?
Flickering shades that glide through grey matter,
Invisible fingers gently tracing the fleshy bedrock of our experiences?

The mind is a haunted house,
Collecting ghosts before being inevitably exorcised of them,
By that kindly priest,
The cruel priest,
Forgetfulness.

His visits grow more frequent,
And with each call paid a ghost,
Beloved or loathed,
Melts away alongside the guttering candles,
Leaving naught but wax and a series of empty rooms
That suit him perfectly well.

One day he will become a fixture of this place, too.

But before he stays,
Indulge your phantoms.
Let them take you by the shivering hand
And guide you safely to familiar places past.

This house…
With its creaking floorboards and crushed hopes,
Leaking faucets and first loves,
Rotten shutters and rich history,
—is as much yours as it is theirs.

And they are eager to share it with you.

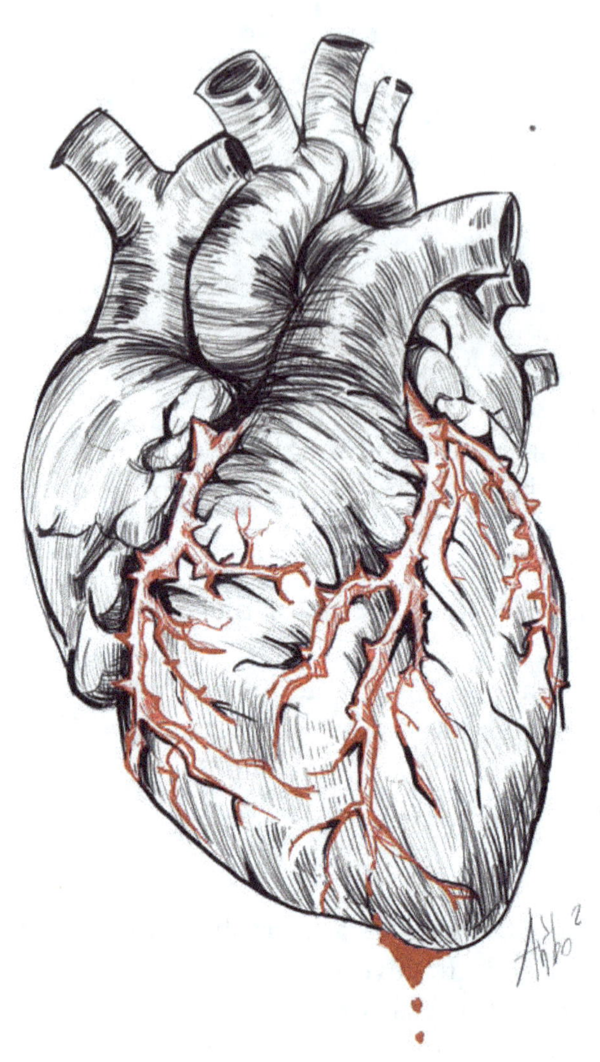

Eryn Hiscock

After Frankenstein

Stuttering synapses
nerves shuddering
lurching momentum
in fits and starts

Some skeletons
six feet under
are less themselves

With recycled eyes
another life flashes
before his
mishmash
mismatch

all thumbs
and two left feet.

No—really:
Two left feet.

He never meant
to kill anyone

—it's just—
once seized—
again—
with life—

He grips too tight.

NEVERMORE!

Terry Campbell

The Crow

On the couch, midnight or later,
Watching American Gladiators
Over a six-pack of beer and a pizza from Domino's.
Laid my head back, almost crashin',
Suddenly there came a smashin'
As of someone loudly bashing,
Bashing in my goddamn door.
"It's the kids," I mumbled, "The kids from next door—
    Only this, ain't no more."

I think it must've been late December
It was cold enough to freeze my member.
The kids must've kicked so hard they blew open the door.
I wished like hell that it was morning,
This same shit was gettin' boring.
Just thumbin' through my Penthouse and Hustler,
Thinking about that freakin' whore.
    She done me wrong, I'll say no more.

But the curtains were a-blowin',
And my hands were nearly frozen.
I could barely turn the pages from one to the next.
But I could see the door still closed,
So why in hell was it so damned cold?
It must've been those little brats from next door.
    That's all it is, ain't no more.

My patience about to reach its end
I stood and grabbed my trusty friend,
An old baseball bat that I used to squash junkyard rats.
"All right. I've had it. This is it.
"Gonna beat your ass, you little shit.
"You'll wish you never,"—I grabbed the door and pulled on it—
    Dark as hell, but nothing more.

I peered through the pitch,
Trying to see,
But nothin' was there and I had to pee, so I slammed it shut and
    headed to the bathroom door.
The naked pictures had got me goin'
Despite the cold wind that still was blowin',
And I found my mind wanderin' back to that old whore.
    Get out of my head, come back no more.

It was hard to get the old boy drainin'
Because it now was surely straining,
Growin' and stretching and tryin' to stand on end.
I reached down and grabbed it in one hand
Takin' myself to the Promised Land,
When I heard the smashin' sound at my door again.
    "Perfect timin' kids—Damn!"

Zipped it up and ran for the door
Grabbed the bat and squeezed it some more,
But the only thing there was a junkyard Crow.
Could it have been making all that noise?
Or was it really those nuisance boys?
But I knelt to the ground to see what the Crow had, rolling
    around like a toy.
    My stomach did then begin to boil.

I stood back up, bent over, threw up
Thought I'd keep going 'til my time was up,
All the while the Crow stared at me with its three beady eyes.
The Crow only had two,
But the third one was blue,
And big and round like a certain whore I knew.
    A whore I once loved, but one who was through.

How did the Crow come by this eye?
And was it the one that I made cry?
And if it had this eye, could the other crows have the rest?
This was not good, I sighed
For crows can fly very high,
And far and wide and drop things here and there.
    Oh, where is the rest of her now, oh where?

But the Crow just stood there,
Spoke two words, cold and bare.
These words that had fluttered in and out of my mind for days.
It jerked its head back,
Gulped the eye like a snack
Then the Crow lowered its eyes and stared at me hard once more.
    I knew those words—"Freakin' whore."

It was someone's idea of a joke, quite sick
If anyone saw I'd take to them a stick,
But it was probably just a trick learned by Morley Fitzer's new pet.
A couple of words,
That his wife surely heard,
Every day of her miserable, chain-smoking, soap-watchin' life.
    "Yeah, that's what it is. Ain't no more."

I grabbed a beer bottle
This bird I would throttle,
And smashed it to amber pieces in front of the Crow.
Its wings flapped and bent,
And I knew what they meant
These words the Crow uttered, these words that I'd spent.
    When I saw the cheap ring again to lament.

It was still on her finger,
And memories linger,
Just as the finger bounced and bobbed from the Crow's piss-
    yellow beak.
I saw the red polish
She wore when she frolicked,
And went out and drank beer and screwed guys other than me.
    Put an end to that when she just wouldn't see.

It was her own fault
The blame is mine naught,
For I told her what would happen if she ever did it again.
I begged and I pleaded,
But the whore just repeated
The acts that rotted my brain and forced my own hand that morn.
    "She'll do those things, nevermore!"

Then I thought the air grew smelly
Made rolls dance inside my belly,
And I wanted nothing more than for the Crow to fly away, finger
    and all.
"Git your ass!" I yelled at it.
"And don't come back, you piece of shit!
"And don't go sniffing under that mattress in the junk pile for
    food no more."
    But the Crow just smiled, "Freakin' whore."

"Bastard!" I yelled. "Stinking bird."
But I had to know where he'd heard the words,
These words that I'd shouted dozens of times that morn.
"Where did you find the eye and the ring?
You really shouldn't bother those things."
And I begged and I pleaded for the Crow to just fly away.
    It smiled, "Nevermore. Freakin' whore."

But I knew even though I continued to yell
This bird had discovered my own private hell,
And had pecked and pulled and now it was part of its own.
But I wanted to know from the bird's own mouth
Was this the one that I'm now without?
And will the words "freakin' whore" ring in the junkyard
    throughout?
    "Freakin' whore, evermore!"

"Go back to the junkyard,
"Or from wherever you came,
"And never again repeat that name, that name that I'll say from
    here on nevermore!
"Leave no black feathers!
"Leave no bird shit!
"Get yer beak outta here and away from my door!"
    Quoth the Crow, "Nevermore."

And the Crow, never flitting,
still is sitting, sometimes shitting
on the branches of the trees just outside my door.
Every day the Crow still brings
Things that remind me of that name,
The other eye, more fingers, bones, or just chunks of meat. The
    freakin' whore's still with me—Evermore!

Mark Tulin

The Rest Stop

I found a rest stop

at the intersection

of the Arizona sun

where the restrooms

were clean,

the hand-sanitizers

were full,

and the sky was bright yellow.

The tumbleweeds

rolled and drifted.

It was a desert nirvana,

a breeze from the north,

a beer to quench my thirst,

but like all drifters who lament,

I felt the twist of a reptile's tongue,

a hiss and a slither,

and the bite of a rattler—

a most unfriendly gift.

M. Brandon Robbins

Heart. Ache.

A bone-white moon
and a candle's flame

Whispering wind of
an autumn night

Chattering rain
blood-red roses bloom

Pricked fingers
on thorns

Two glasses of wine
breathing—

Shivering—
cold as
it once was
in December.

I reach out for
your hand
there is only
dust

Murray Eiland

Broken Window

She gazes out from her shadowed room,
Where moonlight softens the garden's bloom.
A tangle of wildness, fair yet forlorn,
A beauty that mocks her life, outworn.

Her days are drowned in a smothering pall,
No footsteps echo within her hall.
Her playthings—abandoned—lie dust-
     entombed,
Yet her spectral eyes are not yet consumed.

Each night she waits by the crumbling pane,
Her hand outstretched to the silent lane.
She dreams of a face, a voice, a sign,
And longs to escape this lonely confine.

Framed by the stone of her crumbling keep,
A silhouette haunts where the darkness doth
     seep.
Once grand halls now ruin, with silence as
     warden,
Save a ghost and her yearnings, 'midst the
     desolate garden.

Gregory M. Thompson

The Lighthouse Keeper

The fog rolls in, thick as sin
a keeper stirs with a flask of gin.
Ghostly cries drift through the haze
the dead still lost in their ocean graves.

The Wickie gazes over the sea
terrified of what the sound could be.
He checks the light to give the sight
to the ship approaching in the night.

But hours pass, looking through glass,
no boat finds its way near and past.
Then he glimpses on the horizon
figures gliding on the ocean skin.

This strange vision is confounding
the gin is potent and astounding.
The bottle he tosses, then chest he crosses
since he caused those haunting losses.

Shrieks and howls from spectral jowls
a storm of rage, and vengeful growls.
Then the words that he most feared
slammed against the keeper's ears.

"You left us to the rocks that night,
our calls drowned by your drunken blight.
Now keep your light, for none shall see—
we'll drag you down to the blackened sea."

Matt Dennison

Occasion

Theirs was not a ghost story per se—
the old couple would never have stood for that.
But they were dead and sore confused
by locks and such, wind in the hands
that could not grasp no matter how slow
the approach, mirrors, and the arrogant
strangers in their house. "Surely they can
see us," they would mutter to themselves,
sitting on the beds of the intruders as they
shifted in their sleep. They shouted into
the ears of the grownups, lowered their
faces over the lips of the children and blew
mightily, stirring nothing but their own
annoyance and doubts. Commands
and invective were ignored. Obscene
displays were attempted and abandoned,
for they simply walked through each other:
one hugging the curtains, the other stroking
a tulip. Banging on walls and floors was also

no good, for they could find no surface willing
to be struck by the likes of them. Off-key
singing and the rattling of pans were equally
impossible, they soon realized, and shrugged,
sour. They took to staring at their hands
on old grey sheets until they grew faint.
Then at each other. Then back to their hands.
Whole days were consumed in this manner,
where they learned they had neither bones nor
names, heat nor taste, only the air of everlasting
occasion as under the house in a low, minor key,
an old cat told a Chinese tale—eyes closed,
mouth near dirt, she droned on and on
to the delight of her young. This they heard
and did not wish to howl upon. With eyes slowly
closing, lips pursed as if to kiss time, that time
once more… Well, if sleep would have them,
they would go.

Stephen McQuiggan

Involtuation.

What secrets does this doll secrete—
Dark limbo with a dash of Hell?
What knowledge sneers its painted lips
And why can I, its Maker, not tell?
Sculpted from alimentary bolus,
Crowned with a lock of your ratty hair;
I'll disembowel that gutless straw
And start again if I only dare.
Perhaps to pluck out your eye
And stitch its lifeless malice
Directly onto dolly's face
And make your skull her airy palace,
Lay her on your feathered brain
Wrap her up in your countless sins:
Or just make *you* my living doll,
Plunge your heart all full of pins.

J. Weintraub

Halloweens Past

Demons, monsters, vampires, wolves—
masks, all removed once the rounds
have been made, the candy, ghouls
all dispersed, and children arrive
home, gifts in hand, safe and sound.

But for some—like razors inside
the polished fruit—betrayal and fear
reside at home, and year-by-year,
inch-by-inch, sutured to bone
and carved to flesh, the mask adheres.

Sutures like thorns, overgrown
soon with a life of its own,
the normal years, a casual face;
yet still the mask remains behind
the fearful eyes, still fixed in place,
a tethered rage, forever blind.

Jeff Oliver

Apocalyptic Sun

Through this sacrifice, all I can see is my broken heart.
This pain that I feel leaves me with daily scars.
Like a scorpion molting in the desert winds, my suffering pierces
    through me.
Like an apocalyptic sun scorching my skin, my anguish consumes me.
I am exhausted and weak.
I am in a constant state of confusion.
I am cold and unaware, overwhelmed and crazed.
These thoughts are incredibly frightening;
They are so dark and intense, devoid of any light.
I have been pleading and am in desperate need of help.
It is *so* difficult to fight.
I have been constantly under attack from everything that exists here;
Everything bites.

If I could be free from this pain, I would banish it far away.
I would cast it into the void and silence all accompanying noise.
I am reaching out into the vast expanse of the universe.
Please, release me from these chains.
I long for someone to possess the keys to help me escape.
I plead for someone to purify my skin and eradicate the acidic rain.
Please, wash it away.
Please, cast it into the fire where the creatures await.
Madness exemplifies what insanity reveals,
While chaos illuminates what we conceal.
Amidst the flames, our consciousness is at stake.
What awaits in the shadows only seeks to take.

The agony evokes, the tears that cannot be wiped away.
The distress resounds, the melodies that remain unplayed.
The suffering resembles a scorpion molting in the desert winds.
The anguish echoes, the turmoil that can no longer be contained within.
The silence screams, the lyrics that cannot be sung.
The shadows continue to rotate the cylinders—the chamber,
Of the remorseless phantom's gun.
The skin dissolves, falling away in the presence of an apocalyptic sun.

HELP
ME

Ian Bain

I Am a Human Nesting Doll

My s(kin)hell is withered and worn, battered and torn.
If only I could have another
chance, I'd remove the bloody knife
that I plunged into my brother.

The younger me still lives inside.
Just open what Mother'd sewn.
But there's no seam 'round my belly,
so, I make my own.

The knife from my brother's back,
is still sharp,
My old skin parts easy
like the gutting of a carp.

My skin is just like a snake's,
I tell myself. It makes
it easier when the
blood spills.

—

I am a human nesting doll. The last doll.
I lay on the floor, a bloody skeleton, naked metatarsus
my organs and tissues and sinews exposed to the rank air,
and all around are the regretful dolls, removed, horrific catharsis.

I Am a Human Nesting Doll

Blayne Waterloo

Leashed

Today, I untie my ribbon. Let
My head roll—it's been set
Well enough for a while now.
I'll be a set of shoulders and a
Quiet menace for a spell, allowing
Others to fuss and figure it out.
I don't hear a thing, and it allows
Me to feel the air I've been
Walking through. A thick soup of
Promise and solidarity. It pools in
My palms to spread like margarine
On all that touches me, feeds me.
Without a mouth that counts, I derive
Sustenance from my ability to rest
These hips in the ground and recharge.
Muster up the gumption to set my
Head back on, ribbon tied taut.

Krys S Achrem

Please Give Me Scissors

I despise events before breakfast.
Early morning.
The rumbling of my stomach.
Obligations.
Petty, decorated ceremonies with pretty balloons
I can't find my family in the crowd of faceless
    mannequins in caps and gowns.
Heat stroke.
Hallucinating. Sounds and people leaving.
Walking toward an already crowded parking lot.
Before everyone was going to leave.
Shouting.
Angry phone call.
"What are you doing?"
"You always want attention, don't you?!"
Crying.
"It's not always about you."

Years pass.
My dad's service at church.
Early morning.
I miss him.
They mispronounce his name.
We all crowd into a car.
I'm hungry.
I can't think about my grief.
Who are these people?
We arrive.
"How did he die," someone asks
"He died at work,"
Someone who watched his corpse be pulled out of
    the room he died in replied.
I'm aware death does not discriminate.
I told them the truth.
"I thought he died in the bathroom there,
I said. I mean,
Death does not care where you are.

We are husks of meat piloted by electricity
Who make up rules about what is and isn't
    appropriate to say.

She swiftly corrects me.
I didn't know I was supposed to stretch the truth.
She accused me of lying for years,
So I had to tell the truth, didn't I?
Which lies are correct for me to say.
WHY CAN YOU LIE AND I CAN'T?!?!

I get home.
She's furious.
She confronts me.
"GIVE YOUR DAD SOME RESPECT,"
She says.
Slams the door.
I break every one of my plastic coat hangers.
I hit myself,
Punch myself,
Put a pillow over my face,
And I think of writing this poem,
Specifically the line:

I want to die
In a bathroom
Because I don't want dignity to come
With my death

I am worthless.
Just a pawn
That's made to lie,
And accused of it
When telling the truth.
I feel my nose getting longer
And I need some air.
I open my bedroom window and I jump
Into the pool where I drown,
But I miss

And hit the concrete.
A death that no one read about.
A death that is both violent and needy and selfish,
But needed.
Because puppets. Aren't. People.

And in that moment,
Where they pull my corpse
From the wreckage,
There are strings on me,
And they're around my throat.

Amanda M. Blake

Sins of the Asylum

The fires used to burn
all through the night.
You could set your watch
to the amber glowing bright.
Ashes rained upon the town
if the wind blew just right.

On the mountainous horizon,
the asylum crouches and looms
like a monstrous toad of
turrets, gables—a hundred rooms,
a model of medical sophistication
to hold a hundred tombs.

They all go in
and never come out,
damsels in distress
in hysterical bout,
and madmen filled
with unholy doubt.
Crematorium
to columbarium,
the only way to set
their poor souls free
is to float away, away,
smoke on the breeze.

A shower of crematory ash
means a hailstorm of metal,
precious gold and silver
after the dust settles
from fillings and jewelry
to pawn and to peddle.

Is it suspicious that
the warden wears silk,
or that the patients
drink water instead of milk,
while the good doctors
stir cream among their ilk?

Not enough left of souls
to make a substantial ghost,
yet the screams remain,
and the skies rain cremains
searching for a more
peaceful host.
The neighbors complain
and rail against the insane,
while the councilmen
raise their glasses
in a toast.

Who cares if the
town is haunted
and the money stained
when they can vacation
out on the coast
when the ashes
grow too thick
or the townsfolk
get sick
with the madness
that throws them away
into the fire,
into the fire,
into the vast
funeral pyre
of a fruitful empire
of the dubiously insane
burning away
to nothing
and no one?
Perhaps it's time
for you to stay.

They all go in
and never come out,
damsels in distress
in hysterical bout,
and madmen filled
with unholy doubt.
Crematorium
to columbarium,
the only way to set
their poor souls free
is to float away, away,
smoke on the breeze.

Rob MacWolf

This Poem is Haunted

This is the house that he built out of breath.
That was his living. This is his death.
These are his clothes, though he needs them no more.
Those were his shoes, left outside the door.
These are peeled grapes, but pretend they're his eyes.
These are his teeth of unusual size.
This is his hopefulness, quite atrophied,
And that's just the wind, a-whistling outside.
This is a message. Perhaps meant to be
Received by somebody, posthumously.
This is his altar to unheard-of gods.
Here did they hear him. What are the odds?
This is his heart that they carved out of wood.
This is his body. This is his blood.
These are the words that are left of his mind,
And that is the sky he is somewhere behind.

William Shaw

When Shall We Three Meet Again?

i) In Thunder

remorseless movement

from hand to blood-stained hand:

god save the king!

ii) Lightning

the professor, disappointed

by leaf-brimmed hats in the dingy footlights,

begins rethinking

iii) Or in Rain

the witches vanish

into the churning battle-ground;

other meetings to attend

Anna McCluskey

Drip

You can no longer hear the blood dripping.
You lift your head, tangles falling across your face,
blocking your vision in the already dim cellar.

Your hair is so long now. When did it get so long?
You always kept it short, like a proper gentleman.

You push the matted, greasy web away with your free hand,
tucking it behind your ears as best you can,
wincing as your filth-crusted fingers touch a cut on the top of
    your left ear.

You hold your breath, hold yourself entirely still and silent,
listening for the…drip…drip…drip…
that has been your background music for so long,
the rhythmic splatter your only companion for at least two days.

Your lips curl back, baring your teeth in what could have been a
    smile,
long ago, when smiles were part of your reality.

It could be argued, you think, that the person
from whom the blood was dripping was the companion.

But a companion is someone to interact with,
someone whose voice you can hear,
and her tongue was ripped out days ago, her spirit broken long
    before that.

You haven't thought of her as a companion in ages.

The sense of camaraderie, of companionship,
only returned when they cut into her and began the slow, audible
     drip of blood.
It distracted you from the ravings of your own half-broken mind.

They must have given her something, some potion or elixir,
perhaps a salve they spread on the wound.
Something stopped the gash from closing, stopped the blood
     from clotting.

It simply…dripped.
Dripped.
Dripped.

And now it has stopped.
You crawl toward her, instinctively,
your need to know overcoming the awareness that you cannot
     reach her
through the bars that separate your cells.

Nevertheless, you drag yourself across the floor as far as you can
     get.
As close as you can get.

Your chain stops you, as you knew it would, tugging at your wrist.
Still, you inch forward, your disused shoulder muscles protesting,
agony all-encompassing as you stretch your arm back.

And you peer between the iron shafts, squinting with your good
    eye into the gray distance.
She hangs there, a limp shadow, unmoving.

You open your mouth to call her name.
A croak emerges, and you choke on it,
coughing until your throat aches and you feel you will never stop
    coughing.

Desperately, you gasp, trying to draw in breath,
your lungs heaving, your entire body convulsing with the effort.

And at last, your breath quiets.
Still shaking, you inexorably return your attention to the other cell.

She has not moved, not reacted even slightly to your spasms,
your cacophony of respiratory effort.

You close your eye.

Rachel is dead.

You are the sole remainder.

You can only be next.

Akis Linardos

When You Space Out, I Take Control

You plucked the first hair, birthed me inside your mind
Like your life, your scalp a bleeding desert, every leftover
  strand more tempting
You pinched, twisted, stretched, craving that pinprick
  tingle
Bit keratin strands to busy teeth and tongue
No hair left (and no friends either, but who needs
  those?)
You pinch your skin, squeezing harder than ever before
Something pokes between the pores
Something blooms with viscous blood
This is no hair, but a vein pumping your heart
Maybe you'll unravel like a knitting ball. But you won't
  even know
When you space out, I take control
So grab that yarn, and slowly pull

Edward Lodi

Meet the Monsters

Psycho

His loves were mixed up with his hates.

He did strange things to his dates.

He liked to put on

The guise of his Mom—

A regular cut-up, that Bates.

Dracula

The count! So ancient, yet crude.

Undead, but hopelessly lewd.

A creature most sanguine

When sinking his fangs in

A lady both buxom and nude.

Altered Ego

Said Dr. Jekyll to Mr. Hyde:
"What a hassle having you inside!
If we split in two
I'll be rid of you."
They did. He was. Then he died.

King Kong

An unfortunate ape named Kong
had ideas that were morally wrong.
He wanted his way
with actress Fay Wray
but his notion was simply too long.

Dr. Frankenstein's Monster

Embroidered with stitches and creases,
He's a wonder that never ceases:
A menace at large
This human collage
Comprised of bits and pieces.

Delana Luna

Cabin Fever

I can't think my way
out of a corner,
so I'm listening to
            the things
that live in the walls.
They are busy in the dark.
Hunting, feeding, fucking…
It's all very healthy.
Sustainable.

Perhaps they string
Fairy lights
            over
little stuffed feather beds,
made from the skins
of the birds they eat.

In the daytime,
While they sleep in a furry helix,
I move more softly about the house,
Every creak of a board is a splinter
In my spinal cord.

A blooming of a critical worm,
Burrowing into my conscience.
Stay small, stay quiet,
Don't wake them up…

I forget who I'm thinking of;
is it ratty royalty,
small gods in crawlspaces,
thin things that inhabit dark cracks?

All I know is

I don't want them to be disturbed.

Nancy Byrne Iannucci

Brother

I hope you will come with the boys.
The air is clear here,
a clean stream will flow
up their noses.
There are two cats to play with.
I don't think they've seen cats.
Earth is only a year old to them.
They don't have much Earth.
They can play on mine, there's plenty of it.
The corn has grown so high, you should see
    it.
I don't think you've ever seen it.
If it's a windy day, they can watch the stalks
in a Lakota dance and run naked, like Lord of
    the Flies.
They will see a place full of green.
Fresh fruit will ripen for them.
I heard Santino doesn't like bananas;
he gets that fear from you,
but Monte will eat anything.
Won't you come to see me?
Don't let them get that fear from you.

Henry Corrigan

𝔶𝔬𝔲 𝔞𝔫𝔡 𝔶𝔬𝔲𝔯𝔰 𝔞𝔯𝔢 𝔐𝔦𝔫𝔢

picture for Me
the Man of My dreams
pretty please

make Him
perfectly normal
and familiar

make Him your
Father or Uncle
or even your Friend

whatever you
dream or aspire
to be

good
now
picture a woman
and make her

no never mind
she doesn't matter
just make her
whatever you wish

yes that's it
now
turn them loose in Me

let them
walk the streets
make Him take her
by the hand

hear her ask
"where are we going?"
and tell me you don't love
the way she says it

so meek so hopeful
and a bit apprehensive
not wishing to disturb
or offend

"hush you"
He says
smiling sweetly
"don't spoil the surprise"

He pulls her along
and I bring the shadows
the lowering gloom
I blacken the alleys for him

"where are you taking me?"
she tries again
fearful but not crying
not yet

"hush I said!"
He replies
forcefully
"Stop spoiling this for me"

she looks for help then
and it *is* there
the doors are listening
and the windows all have eyes

but will *you* help her?
I hope not
I'm not done
with her yet

oh *thank you*
you are
too kind to Me
I swear

she tries to run then
because who wouldn't
but He has such a grip
this Man you made

"please I want to go home!"
she cries
digging in heels
that break beneath her

"HUSH!"
He howls
dragging her now
by the hair

she screams and even this
is a real gift
because the doors won't listen
and the windows stay shut

her voice could shatter
the ground He walks on
but I don't even have to
deaden the sound

because once He drags her in
she's Mine
and once He strolls out
He is too

I may be darkness
but this Man is *ruination*
and I love Him
down to his red red grin

now
if I could ask
for just
one more thing

make another one
for Me
make *more* of Him
for Me

pretty please

Linda M. Crate

& they would die

the witch wanted
her revenge,
she had lost her daughters
to men who were angry
with their loss;
men who blamed her because
her potions and spells,
when all she had ever tried to do
was to help them and their wives—

she had cautioned both women that
they would not survive childbirth,
but they refused to heed her warning;

they both died—

& so the men thought they'd teach
her a lesson,
but she was innocent and blameless in this;

yet the witch also had a temper
black as night and hot as hell—

she made a spell with her daughter's bones
that would curse any who slandered her
or their name;
that they would see her and her daughters
in their nightmares, but those dark dreams would
be their reality & they would die.

John Grey

𝕬 𝔚inter of the 𝔖oul

It's a winter's night,
wind from the north,
hangman's rope swinging,
skeleton rattling in the window
of Doc Jacob's potions store.
And so much darkness,
deep and unwavering.

The world is reduced to sounds,
the clip of shoes on a sidewalk,
the drag of wheels through snow,
the bat's deep dive into the trees,
the distant wolf choir.

Life is in its inevitable decay,
with every bough stripped of foliage
and a chill freezing blood-flow
to and from the heart.

It's a time for believing in nothing,
for feeling God's abandonment,
fearing that children are as likely
to be gleaned by the reaper
as an old man in his nineties.

Expressions are universally pale and dour.
Humor is written by and for the graveyard.
Statues in the park
are as alive as the drunkards
sprawled shivering at their stone feet.

There is no evading doom.
The life that once was a cycle
is now a straight line
that ends in fog and dirt.

It's the winter of the closing in,
the narrowing of fortune.
You may not die of it,
but your living won't recover.

AJ Bartholomew

Amber Eyes

Listen closely to words from the wise

Keep away from fields with amber eyes

From down below

You'll see their glow

Run away quick before monsters rise.

Hannan Khan

Eternity

Crossing the graveyard…
The murmuring sad echoes—
Vastness of silence.

Would I be able…
to feel that touch, love, and care—
lying deep in clay?

The wilting flowers on the barren domes…
    the haunting memories…the flickering
    shadows dancing like reverse film…
    whispering sighs, thoughts zoning in a
    drowsy mind…the untouched mirages…

Perhaps not, not ever.
As the dead never came back
They walk where time fades—

Lillian Csernica

Evil Sirens Sweetly Singing

Wake to the world of the darkness
Wake to the world of the Night.
Burn with the fires of Hecate
Ache with the Devil's delight.

Live in the land of Jung's shadow
Dance in the mind's shady gloom
Dive into Charon's black waters
Swing on the bell-rope of doom!

Hark to the Muse of the Lethe
Smash sanity's last painful shard
Revel with your nightmare secrets
Give voice to the soul's darkest bard.

Cry with your soul's hundred voices
Fling wide the crypt in your heart
Bathe in the hungers within you
Damnation is only the start!

Ron Schroer

Hammer Horror

Hammer,
Hammer's horror,
cheap and lurid,
a penniless aristocrat
feeding off old graves.
Yet some things endure
and live on, in a way.

God bless Count Dracula,
noble and persistent,
rising above the dreck
of his surroundings,
red eyes
looking for a virgin's blood
and some good old-fashioned vengeance.

Bela's ring on his finger,
his cape a princely winding sheet,
this regal, handsome Count
seeks the quiet
of a crumbling castle
or the chill
of a desanctified church.

And who could blame him?
Why should he care
about the passage of time
and a world on the move?
Old haunts and classic motives suit him;
between murders I think he reminisces
about a shaded, royal past.
In his world
his clothes are always perfect,
his slicked-back hair ruffled
only by the latest Van Helsing
barging in to shed light
on a timeless corruption.
Insolent meddler!

"My revenge has spread over centuries
and has just begun!"

Defiant to the end
he fights to live
and always dies,
the common struggle.
But this cold man,
even dead on the stake,
has an edge:

Ashes to ashes, dust to dust,
he lies waiting for the call,
rising from his bed, the earth.
What uncommon luxury,
to live and live again,
to look with disdain
on another new world.

Dear Van Helsing is dead now
and the House of Hammer
a boarded-up ruin
held together by nostalgics like me.
But the Prince of Darkness,
above us all,
is unconcerned.

Nice work if you can get it.

Hailey Samford

Literal

There's a hand in my chest
Literal
And not figurative

One has to be concise about these matters
Lest some scholar
Years later on
Starts to cut into you

And says
'Look, youngsters, look
'Look at how the mighty have fallen
'Look at how his childhood
'Shaped him against his will

'Look at how the hand symbolizes
'Immaturity
'Weakness
'Being made a pawn'

I do not want that scholar to think as such
To think that the father that did not shape me
Had any literal or figurative hand in the
        raising of me
And that the mother who had
Did such a bad job
That there's now a hand in my chest
Literal
And not figurative
And that it was her fault

Right
The hand
It's in my chest
Literal
And not figurative

The person it's attached to is
Well
Doesn't matter
It's in my chest
Mine
And mine
Alone

Digging out my heart
Buried under bone
Under sinew
Under veins
And lungs
And walls of iron
And teardrops that fall
And bristling anger
And sharp sharp sharp sharp teeth

There's a voice talking
Are they sad?
Angry?
Happy?
That their hand
Is in my chest
And my life sputters out around their wrist?

Literal
And not figurative

It doesn't matter
It doesn't
What's done is done

And as my knees strike the floor
As the hand in my chest—
Literal
And
Not
Figurative—
Claws itself free

I think for a moment

That it all seems far too fa—

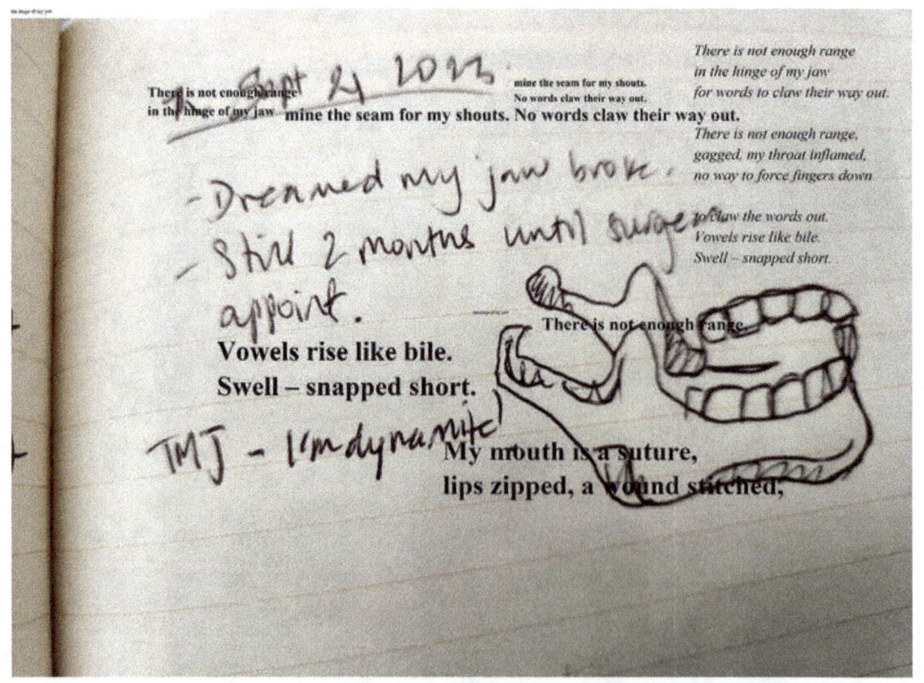

J. J. Munro

Idi Amin's Brain

It must be sitting in
a jar
          somewhere
nobody would simply
burn it
or bury it
or consume it

would they?

unless there wasn't
a jar big enough
to hold

                    it

JJ Carpenter

I Am Haunted

I sense their ever-present stares, which seem to snare me in their
 glares,
And set upon me when at my most beaten and exhausted.
They grin and peek and flutter, under their breaths I hear them
 mutter.
But all I can achieve is stutter, as beneath contorted stares I stand
 so taunted.
For surely, it is I who is now haunted.

If only they were from the past, but not from history they're cast,
They make themselves known from inside their human host.
I am not any kind of resurrector, or summoner of spooky spectre,
It's they I sense are the collector, and it's me with whom they're so
 engrossed.
It is I who is their prize-ed ghost.

Do they come here from the future? Ripped through time, no
 thought to suture,
The rip they've made across and through our space and time?
Come back from some era far away, casting our hist'ry in disarray,
Is it me who loops 'round on replay, like some poor and voiceless
 mime?
A skint puppet in some play sublime?

I must describe their many faces, across all creeds and age and
     races,
All screw their eyes, and pinch their lips, like on the brink of
     tantrum.
They gape, they stare, they preen, all expressions lit and keen,
As though I'm a sight rarely seen, and they're my biggest fandom.
Am I their ghoulish, moppet phantom?
Am I the ghost then, haunting them? In limbo have I been
     condemned,
Sentenced to replay my successes, failure, pain and love until I
     scream?
Have they not come back to the past, but simply me adrift am
     cast,
My misery and sentence passed, no idea of how I can redeem?
Is it mine, or their, unending dream?

Not all of our mind is yet known, I feel their must be hidden
     zones,
They say we never lose our memories once gained.
If that is true, can some far person, use some still unknown
     exertion,
Of a future genius surgeon, to send a person back again?
To relive a memory reobtained?

And what if I should stand up in defiance, of this unsettling,
     twisted science,
That has made their past, my present and future all distorted?
What did I do to hold their ire, or perchance did I inspire?
Could they seek what they admire when into times past they're
     transported?
Yes indeed, it is I who is now haunted.

I am haunted.

Odin Meadows

Shuck

It's that time of year again. The corn, near death, is ready for harvest at any moment, and that far too familiar feeling floats above my head like an anvil, threatening to drop. Hopefully, this time, I can slip into an amniotic depression, one where I can fashion an umbilical noose and rebirth myself, shucking my old-self, revealing a Brand New projection of my perceived inadequacies that shines like an over-wattaged bulb

but

my old-self clings to my heels like a grisly shadow that chuckles in the night as it pools around my ankles, tangling itself in the sheets. I toss and turn, try to kick it off, but it sticks to me, attached by the Achilles. I try to chew it off. I grind with my molars, mouth full of blood, mouth sore. I grind.

I grind.

Lily Black

The Claim

My long black dress drags behind
me along the stone pavement.
It's richly ornate, darker
than the starless night sky
spread above me.
Veil over my face,
it gives me refuge
from the intrusive world
and inevitable fate.

Lightning cleaves the heavens
as I push the chapel's heavy door
open.
I enter, leaving
my previous existence behind.
I have no choice in this.
He demanded to claim me
and I have no power
to decline.

The door falls shut, cutting me off
from everything I know.
In this plane, he and I alone
exist.
He comes, lifts my veil.
I gaze into his eyes.
I see the final sunset
reflected in them,
as well as a timid crack of dawn.

I look beyond that,
and I find
both source and reprieve
from anguish.
I see a river,
myriads of lost souls.
I will not be lost, though.
I come willingly,
to be found.

He offers his hand
and I accept.
His touch pierces my skin,
engulfs my whole body,
grips my heart.
I have no power to decline,
so I surrender
to an end
and a beginning.

Em Arata-Berkel

Is Something Wrong

When I ask,
        you become
An animal
        before headlights.
You keep your
        doe eyes dark, but

They gape for me—
        twin mawkish caverns
To our hollowed souls,
        in which we keep sour milk things
Buried somewhere between
        time-sharp, stalagmite teeth.

You don't answer;
        you tinker instead,
Pick your words
        like mousy bones loose,
Place them in my hands,
        and fold yours beneath
A rabbit-sweet chin.

You wait for me
        to swallow what's yours,
Open my mouth full,
        and give you mine.

J. Agombar

Trail Gone Cold

On lamp posts and cars
In a small Alaskan town
Missing posters stick

Forlorn eyes read on
Doubting she is still alive
After the last two

For the people know
There is a killer in town
A roaming monster

For the evil mind
The woods are always the key
To hiding a soul

Nature is beauty
But is always the hardest
To find a victim

Detectives glance up
Helicopter flies above
Pilot gives signal

Pilot flies ahead
Needles twitch and pine trees sway
Infrared and lights

They enter the woods
A blanket of snow beneath
crunches underfoot

Kind volunteers and
Police accompany them
Leaving nothing but

Hopeful thoughts and
Myriad footprints behind
They advance in line

A covert killer
Proves the most devious mind
To trace in small towns

They make you question
The barman? Or the banker?
The teacher? The vet?

Superstition reigns
Among the community
Who thought itself tight

A tree is approached
A symbol scratched upon it
Dark gloves touch the bark

Blood stains the carving
A familiar sigil
Unsettles the nerves

A triskelion
The three interlocking horns
The Cult of Odin

Horror lies beyond
The body of the young girl
Only seventeen

Crimson upon white
The message is clear to all
But lacking reason

No need to check pulse
The ferryman has claimed her
Taken far too young

Somebody's sister
Someday somebody's mother
Somebody's daughter

Three sacrifices
All among the frosted pines
Hail to dark intent

The mantic knowledge
That Odin sought from the gods
They think they'll attain

Snow falls rapidly
Nature holds a cruelty
Conceals the footprints

The search is halted
Flames of hope dwindle in white
With the evidence

Families accuse
Out of pain to no avail
Tempers become high
Leads are followed up
Homes are raided in error
Resources wasted

Has the killer fled?
Do they still walk among us?
Is there merely one?

Cults make their own rules
Is it control or knowledge?
Snow melts and leaves grow

Spring arrives in time
Beauty hides horror once more
But not memories

Another season
Passes with no solid path
Evidence is weak

Sorrow will replace
Anger in time, along with
Too many questions

The bereaved, just like
The detectives, feel at loss
But life carries on

Reluctant, they made
The unsettling call to say
The trail had gone cold

Corinne Pollard

See Here

Shadows dwell here,
hidden in monochrome;
where black paints
and white suffocates.

Shadows grin here.
They dwell in the windows,
upside down,
peering at their view;
where the moon bends its smile,
and the stars slash the sky.

Shadows bleed here,
forever watching you,
mute ruins,
shredding over time,
until you catch a glimpse.
Then they lick,
eager to pursue,
and taste your shivers.

Shadows frown here,
waiting in monochrome,
and I'm one of them.

Kelli Dianne Rule

𝕴𝖋

…the cold black blood
and castoffs of gristle
and forgettable bits of flesh
paused their dying and reversed
to pool inward and

moved up from the linoleum
in an other-way funnel cloud
and slicked backwards along
the cleaver's edge and dripped

one by one, single-file, back
into the neck of the pheasant
and the wound, self-stitched and
sealed, and

the feathers laid
flat and the eyes
went wet and
burned with life

would the butcher repent,
carry it back to its nest,
or would he kill it again,
being inherently irreverent?

Nicole Field

The Coming of Persephone

Long has Hecate dwelled beneath the earth,
But also the sky
She is the crossroads,
She is the way,
She is the crossroads.
The path feared to take,
As well as the path chosen
When decisions are made.

(And she can feel it)
She can feel it in the air
(And she can feel it)
She can feel it in the sky
(And she can feel it)
She can feel it in the earth
(And she can feel it)
That earth is going to shake
And quiver
And cry

Like a spider in a web,
Hecate has always been there,
Daughter of the mother of
The night time stars
And the father of destruction.

Change with the times,
Changing with Hecate,
Change in flowering valleys,
Change in the very soul,
That part which makes up
All that will one day go
From the world of the living
To the other one below.
Better be careful,
Better you know,
Things are different now,
Styx and Acheron begin to flow.

The Fates have spoken to her
(And they are not the only ones)
The Erinyes have spoken to her
(And they are not the only ones)
The Beasts have spoken to her
(And they are not the only ones)
They each have called
And now Hecate can answer.

Like a spider in a web,
Hecate has watched,
Has waited, ever swinging
From hope towards total rupture.
These things
Have gossamer wings
Made to look exactly
Alike to one another.

Hecate's hands raise to the sky,
Her feet stomp down the damp earth flesh.
Her hands raise to the stone,
Her feet stomp against dust of all that came before.
"She is coming,"
They call,
Have called,
Are calling.

And it's Hecate's time to answer:
"She *is* coming."
The Queen of Darkness
Is Coming,
The Queen of Light
Is Coming,
The Queen of Spring
Is coming,
The Queen of the Underworld
Is coming.

No…
No longer coming.

She
H A S
C O M E.

Bernardo Villela

In the Distance Dark
(Gargoyle Poem #1)

A shuffling, sinister flight
under cover of the darkling drear,
a winged hellion seeking a fight
within me breeds mounting fear.

The penumbral blood-red night,
its spit-billowed flames do sear
my skin whilst running off in fright,
my burnt ears do his bellows hear.

In the distance dark, more beasts
from the other directions come,
the ember-lit sky down-presses.

Tricked, I am fodder for their feasts.
Conflagrated night, over-glum,
teeth rend me, blood effervesces.

Kyle Nowak

Jaded Lament

This was the death of a once happy Jade.
A corpse among others in the game that she played.
The game itself never came to an end;
And there was only one rule: to simply pretend.

Day by day. Year after year.
Screams from the inside she started to hear.
The screams, they went on. She drove herself mad.
Her thoughts about death were thoughts that were glad.

Jade had continued, ignoring those screams,
Until they had crept into all of her dreams.

Grayness stayed gray. Stillness stood still.
Cadaverous minds controlled against will.

Life had but blurred, it flew right on by.
Her rotting remains only knew how to cry.
Jade had grown old, her being was wrung;
The release of her sorrows in the misery sung.

This was the death of a once happy Jade.
She'll continue in death. Continue…she played.

Katherine Quevedo

Peter Pumpkin Eater's Most Delectable Carving

Armed with handsaw, gouge, and chisel,
Peter Pumpkin Eater toiled
by candlelight 'til his fingers blistered.
Somehow, his pumpkin never spoiled.
He carved in layers, working inward
for greater translucence. Outer rind
gave way to tender, paler, thinner,
wetter flesh. He paid no mind
to the teardrop pumpkin seeds within,
except as more dessert to eat,
like the juice collecting on his fingers,
like the lumps of fibrous pumpkin meat,
like the sour reek of stringy innards,
like the soft resistance of the shell.
He broke her, shaped her, named her, lit her,
and there he kept her very well.

Yelena Crane

Meat in the Machine

The crowd's rock and roll wild
pumped to the psychedelic strumming
of my calloused Jimi Hendrix fingers.
"'Scuse me while…" I'm
Einstein. White hairs frizzed
like hydrogen atoms curving space time.
Mass traded. Speed of light squared in my…
double helix. Credited to Crick and Watson.
Heavy-lifting Acknowledgements.
They forgot to steal the ovarian cancer
that came with my X-ray crystallography.
Call me Rosalind.
I'm all the greatest emperors,
and the lowliest of slaves.
Until the connection blanks
and I am forced to be myself again.
A jellied beast, wasting space,
waiting to escape. Stuck. Trade places?
Please?
I'm…

Gary Every

The Necropoliti

She was pale, silent, and petite,
stunningly beautiful
and she always wore a funeral wreath.
She sustained herself on a diet of
cigarettes, coffee, and red wine
as if she were allergic to fruits and vegetables.
She and the sun were not well acquainted
and they certainly weren't friends.

She wandered the necropolis at midnight,
a member of an elite secret citizenry
known as the Necropoliti,
a mysterious society of ancient scholars
and new-age philosophers.
When the scholars spoke of Roman emperors
it was as if they had broken bread with them,
gotten drunk with Dionysus,
and passed out beneath his table.
Sometimes I thought,
as they talked and talked, spewing bad breath,
that all they wanted was to bore me to death.

This daughter of the dead had big, beautiful, sullen eyes
which danced with light from side-to-side
like a moth circling a flame,
spellbound inside a tragic trance.
To romance her I bought black roses,
which were seen only as shadows in daylight,
and their darkness remained unseen at midnight
but viewed reflected through water,
the ripples revealed the roses' radiance
like viewing the world through eyes
distorted with prismatic tears.
All I sought was one blissful kiss
but how was I to know she wore poison lips?

Kevin David Anderson

Nightmare

Something dark
stalks me in my sleep
It goes where I go
It touches what I touch
It knows what I know
It is just a nightmare, I say
But now it follows me
In the light of day
It lingers in my shadow
Going where I go
Touching what I touch
Knowing what I know
It's so close to me I can feel it breathe
I close my eyes, wishing it away
It doesn't take the hint
It wants to come out and play
It is just a nightmare, I say
I opened my eyes and I finally saw
It has a reflection
Grotesque, haunted, evil
I know it is only a nightmare
One that goes where I go
One that touches what I touch
One who knows what I know
But how, how can this be
And with a cold revelation
I suddenly know
Because the nightmare is me

L.G. Testa

Paradox

A prey bird's squeak,
a seemingly violent gaze through branches,
to which you will answer ignorantly—
no, you won't free her.
Her roar against heaven—
painfully agonized;
still, nothing closes her mind
praying for the whole world,
even the universe.
But you condemn her
because in your frame of mind
she deserved that for strong peculiarity.
Try to break this paradox—
one imprisoned by physical obstacles,
the other—by limited thinking.

FAITH
HOPE
CHARITY

Foong

In the Stillness

Shadows shift and swirl
Fear crawls, thick sinuous ropes
Trapped in the stillness

Silence tastes of blood
Heartbeats slowed, sputtered, snuffed out
No one ever leaves

Shadows shift and swirl
Fear crawls in thick sinuous ropes
Trapped in the stillness
snuffed out
Heartbeats stand No one our bodies
Silence fuses of but
foongsart

LindaAnn LoSchiavo

My Dungeon Ghost

"If ye will listen to me, but for a little
while, I will tell it … in story stiff and
strong…"—*Gawain and the Green Knight*

I.

He gave me my first kiss, a kiss which all
Others aspire to be. But that was not
As memorable as when he crept up
Behind me, deep in the stacks with
Shakespeare, And thrust *Le Morte d'Arthur*
into my life. Uther Pendragon, Lady
of the Lake, La Belle Isolde, Lamorak,
Galahad, Gawain and the Green Knight:
he'd rattle off These names like boys
on our block recited Today's New York
Yankees' starting lineup. Under his spell,
I became capable Of sin, adulteress
wed to the head Of Camelot, while
disreputably Cavorting. He cast me as
Guinevere, Himself as Lancelot, my
illicit Paramour. Troubadours lionized
my Beauty. Fortified by my favor, he
Won all tournaments, adoring his new
Heroic entity, the prison-like Grip of
its shallowness, his eyes askew. Fantasy
twitched, hid its murderous heart. We're
library-eyed sixth graders, bewitched
By British poetry, legends, and lore.
He's eleven years old. I'd just turned
nine. Sundays we'd serve God together,
speaking Liturgical Latin, prim altar
boy In the sanctuary, his Juliet On the
balcony—choir loft—voice raised. "Lead

us not into temptation," we'd sing. In
class we'd pass naughty notes, wild
words penned By Malory, Tennyson, and
Chaucer. He dreamt of noble crusades,
mighty steeds. I thought about what
constitutes the light 'Round which friends
gather, pull each other up. Three years
later, I cast aside wimples, Tippets, and
my power to petition, As Camelot's
queen, for a Papal Bull. The Round Table
was no more, upended. Graduation. New
unknowns descended.

II.

*"Sir Knight, if thou cravest battle here thou shalt not
     fail for lack of a foe."*
There he was on horseback at The Cloisters,
     Preparing to joust, taller, brawnier, More
     Green Knight than Gawain but, all the
     same, A *verray, parfit, gentil knyght.* No
     words Passed. *His baner desplayeth, and forth
     rood.*
When I described his armor to neighbors,
     They derided him: college dropout,
     drunk, An unseemly Port Authority cop.
*"Knight or patrolman, he's a barrier To chaos. Love
     whatever saves your life!"* This sassed retort is
     thought, not said. What nerve. My words
     have more heft than gossips deserve.
Instead I kept my fingers on the pulse
     Of Chaucer, Tennyson, Malory, Bede,
     Chretien de Troyes, and William
     Langland, Earned my degrees by
     forgetting to sleep, Becoming an
     anchoress, books knee-deep.

III.

"Where shall I seek thee?" quoth Gawain.

Decades passed. When his voice returned, as
    if Magnetic force spun a dusty mixtape
    From life's forgotten hits, as if he'd reeled
    Me back to the library's Children's Room,
    As if he were transmitting from the
    spheres, I was too busy to listen at first.
When his voice returned, insistent,
    troubled, It took three weeks before his
    confession Was complete. His crimes
    were unspeakable, Impressed their brutish
    force across the miles.
During the course of a contract murder, His
    cowardice left an infant to starve, Bawling
    inside her crib, though her father Made
    provisions for her safe retrieval From
    this house of carnage. But the killers—
    Two men who'd sired children—did not
    phone.
In air arranged by bees, the final sting Blitzed:
    a slow-witted male was convicted, Stewed
    behind bars for nine years, innocent,
    Incapable of such a heinous crime, While
    my friend refused to speak, let it be,
    Abused his liberty by offering Himself as
    a paid assassin for hire.
Sweet altar boy, who rang the bells during
    Lent's *Miserere*, had turned mercenary.
Arrests came ten years later when he was
    Outed. His partner, ill now, suddenly
    Decided to name the victim's husband
    And him, betraying his accomplices.
Hours spent with the venerable Bede
    Enlightened us to the ways of the world,
    Its fickleness and instability. We valued
    courtly love and *curteisie*. What incited
    moral degradation?
"Ye gan to grucche me!" was his sore
    complaint. Yet he explained how he

sought false glory, A mad pursuit of
   titles—duke and king—Jousting in a
   mirrored colosseum, Betraying himself,
   forever in debt.
Consumed by shallowness, pride, and regret,
   My friend had declined a coherent eye.
To offer him cash, I phoned the prison.

"He's been gone a month," the chaplain
   advised.
"When no one claimed him, inmates dug his
   grave."
"Prithee grant an inestimable boon, My
   queen, whose loyalty's my only hope.
   Family hates me but find my daughter. Say
   I'm very sorry and I love her."
I thought of what the Green Knight told
   Gawain: Kindness, mercy, and what's "less
   than to blame." I pledged fealty. Then he
   said her name.
*A knight ther was and that a worthy man, That
   fro the tyme that he first bigan To riden out, he
   loved chivalrie, Trouthe and honour, fredom and
   curteisie.*

***

Section headings are all from *Gawain and the
   Green Knight.*"
verray, parfit, ..." Chaucer, *The Canterbury
   Tales, General Prologue*, line 72
"His baner desplayath..." Chaucer, *The
   Knight's Tale*, line 966"
A knight ther was ..." Chaucer, *The Canterbury
   Tales, General Prologue*, lines 43-46

Tehnuka

The New Children

after Lucy Clifford

She warned her children
if they were naughty
her eyes would turn to stone.
You can have so much fun
with young imaginations.

Inevitably, lost in play,
they came home
mud-spattered-late-to-tea
and with one look fled in horror.
She laughed,
removed gray contact lenses,
and waited for them to return to her

until that night,
sick-stomached that they hadn't crept back
to peer through the windows,
she found them huddled on the muddy
    streambank.
Rushed to sweep them into her arms,
but they only looked at her
blank,

through river pebbles.
She wept as she carried her poor cold darlings
on the winding forest path
home to their cottage,
apologizing
in words,
tears,
kisses. There,

she reheatcd soup
and the chilled bathwater.

As they thawed
she hoped their eyes would melt,
recognize her,
and mouths open to spoons at their lips.

Their lips did twitch—
but they only muttered garbled syllables she
    barely heard
and only to one another.

She wrapped them in towels
left them staring
as she fetched worn flannel pajamas
and put in her contacts.

Knowing her opaque-eyed,
they finally embraced their mother.
Did it matter to be a stony-gazed family,
if it meant they were together?

Steve Denehan

The Empty Room

There is no heat
in the winter sunlight
that floods the room

in the corner, just inside the door
a young mother nurses her baby
gazing at him, rocking him gently
all of it still new
to both

not far from her sits another woman
middle-aged, her hair upturned
stiffly playing the piano

a young man stands at the window, smiling
one hand held behind his back
the other waving
not quite frantically

an old man walks the width of the room
back and forth, back and forth
near the gable wall
running his hand
through hair, pure white
shoulder length

in the centre of the room
kneels a little girl
her face frozen in fear
beneath her lies a stricken boy
moving in wild jerks
a puppet operated
by a mad puppeteer

the door opens
a young woman enters the room
singing happily to herself
happily, and loudly
striding purposefully
to open a large dresser drawer
utterly unaware
of the other occupants
what with each and every one of them
being long dead

Jonathan Ukah

My Father Dies A Second Time

My father's bungalow
dreamt of eternity
amid the tall red hibiscuses,
luxurious brambles and grass,
daffodils and Chrysanthemum;
hedged in a thicket
of *Eupatorium odorantum*

My father watched over it
from the ivy-covered home,
his granite grave;
where a mesh of red and yellow sun
have built a pyramidal canopy
of spiky spear grasses and shrubs.

As the axe rose over the roof
of my father's ancient bungalow,
I felt him wince and writhe in his grave,
flinch, shove and stagger to the right,
his termite-infested head sagged,
and a lone tear dropped on the daisies.

I landed another blow to the roof,
on the lintel and the decking;
My father's body contorted,
wriggled and convulsed
like a Harmattan-beaten cocoyam,
dead to the music of the living
and the loud sound of dying.

He would not sleep,
he would not stay awake,
for the trauma of another blow,
the crash of pillars and blocks,
the descent into chaos
and how darkness was unrecognised,
was his afternoon nightmares.

The dream of a bungalow
always turns into a nightmare;
by the walls of the duplex,
the rays of the sun blunted
and there was no colour
to the thing that made our dreams.
The moon was a shy girl,
after the bungalow collapsed.

I saw cracks on my father's grave,
like glass crashing on a terrace
or a leaf chunked in bits
by hordes of insects.
They were his lips parting,
his mouth opened in a smile,
his welcome of this growth,
this march towards his dreams,
towards his peaceful rest at last.

Phillip E. Dixon

Oh, toes

bumbling blocks of flesh
covered in black and blue
berry jam filling
crevasse and canvas
bulbous delight
in amber brine
on my shelf
to keep lickable eyes
and kissable teeth
in good company
until cuticles melt
and sizzle and crisp
whorling and whirling
on summer days
in my pan

David Bennett Black

Foraging For Fruit:
A Coward's Poem

*"I was reading the dictionary, I thought it was a poem
about everything."* —Steven Wright

Foraging for fruit, foraging for seed,
Foraging to make the coward bleed.
The lilac here and poppy o'er there,
We've waited so long, this coward so rare.
The thicket is so green, so lush and so true,
A family of vine, father, son, and nephew.
The coward was here and then he was gone,
The judge o'er there, his mind at predawn.
The jackets with guns, their blue vests a plenty,
Their minds dull and dumb, I could have killed twenty.
With no reprise or fear of their incoming steer,
The dolts thought we were oh-so friendly.
Now here I am, forest tall as a cloud,
My ingredients within, ready for the gaping mouth.
The coward hoped within for his shroud.
Waiting for the bubbling, the cauldering sounds.
He isn't the first and won't be the end,
Just like the others, he may not comprehend.
His eyes in the dark, his body tied still,
This one is the coward, warm blood wanting to spill.
The land is still open, my satchel is free,
The greens filled with envy, death on the marquee.
One of fur before skin, the recipe needing,
I catch a small squirrel, her neck nimble and bleeding.
I break off a limb, a hand needed for thee,
A bone in the stew, the spell's first seeding.
The other is gone, will return through this brew,
With the coward's flesh, this coven will grow in lieu.

My satchel full, the recipe ready,
I head for my camp, my duty so steady.
His blood will be poured, his intestines confetti.
Lush to so thin, my fire within,
A cabin stands tall, so small yet so hearty,
my home and my bed, a cauldron and more,
How could I have been so tardy?
To my own house?
To my own spell?
If the coward is dead, all I'll say is—Oh, well.
The flesh should be fresh, the death within minutes,
The magic tells me so, I'm well within limits.
Rusted hinges swing as I enter my home,
If I were a stranger, I'd think I was surely alone.
The fact of the cellar, I gave not one hint,
The secret is mine, not even blueprint.
The sound is well hidden, the screams dialed down,
The villagers so tragic, how close in their town.
Their back-lights still shone, my window bright blue,
They were ever so close, thankfully, I have you.
The book of our spells, some written, some screamed,
Keeps the town mute as I kidnap their dreams.
I unlatch the latch and smell his strong stench,
Why bother to clean him, dirty blood is more quenched.
He whimpers and groans and bemoans my strong tone.
The chain holds him tight, his gag dripping drool,
Below his legs urine, a whole goddamn pool.
The coward not dead, the time comes so near,
I smile as his screaming wet piles to tears.
He knows he will die but not how or the why,
The when is however so present,
The Coward now cries, freedom for lies,
Shall I offer a numbing depressant?
And remove my joy? No way, no how,
The spell will be chorused with shrieking sound,
Music from him, the dying hound.
I exit the hidden, ready to ingest the ridden,
His soul the final ingredient.

My power returns them, the spell is forbidden,
But his body will take the brunt.
I empty my satchel, the plant life aplenty, straight into the boiling pot,
(along with the squirrel, I attest within this journal.)
I deep stab his neck, his life does now drain, his body is ready to rot,
But before rigor mortis, let this now court us
Three souls from the devil, I've bought.
I drink in the potion, the smoothness like lotion,
As my throat feels the caking gin,
No alcohol, I wish that there was,
But here comes the return of their skin.
From the coward's cold corpse, came the three that were lost,
My sisters and me, back at last.
And then came their faces, their lips in mid-beckon.
Words of thanks filter through, as they grew all their sections.
I followed the birth, the man's corpse now rotten stew,
My maidens, my friends, returned to me anew.
Dead for some years, the coward's blood was the answer,
With them returned—look at us, take a gander.

Lee Clark Zumpe

Poor Little Fellow

Poor little fellow, so obedient and mild—
he never took exception to my capricious moods,
and afforded me devoted attention
and unconditional affection.
Such an appalling and unexpected tragedy—
finding him in this sad state,
robbed of his vigor and vivacity,
woefully denied the dignity of a speedy demise.

Only this morning, he seemed so full of life:
sitting at the kitchen table,
enjoying toast and scrambled eggs
while scowling strangers gibbered at each other
inside the magic box in the living room—
the one he leaves on for me, as if I take interest
in their monotonous narrative.

Though lately, the content did attract my gaze:
scenes depicting acts of savage violence—
even more alarming than those shown most days—
played in a grisly loop as commentators
uttered words both familiar and meaningless:
virus, plague, pandemic, cannibals, zombies.

Now, having stirred from my midday nap,
this ghastly vignette greets me:
his skin has turned an ashen gray,
his eyes are milky and distant.
He is hunched over an elderly neighbor
like some lone vulture over its carrion meal,
stubbornly working to tear flesh from bone.

He peers at me curiously:
his bloodied face twists and contorts,
reflecting some dull aspect of recognition;
a wistful memory of his sable-coated companion,
rescued from starvation years ago
from an abandoned warehouse on the edge of town.

Panicked voices continue to stream
from the magic box for several days,
and then the house falls into a long, still silence.

Klaus Iliff Hageman

The "Ballad" of Talamah Loch

In a place of mist and woe we land
Of humid boughs of oaks moss-draped
Whither shades of those loved and hath lost yet roam
And the living still weep for a grief not escaped

Those who hath lost someone dearly beloved
Though they may hast fled that land long ago
Find themselves drawn back thither in dreams
To chase their lief spectres and the shadows they throw

Endlessly wandering the exsufflicate brick roads
Peeking 'round corners for a glimpse of their love,
Feel terror creep closer with each futile step,
Grasp for lights in darkness and find absence thereof

Each dream seems more hopeless as time goeth on
The streets grow ever longer and more winding each night
When longing pulls desperates to the true ground for searching
They find only new sorrows that add to their plight

For this is the nature of earthly goods and pursuits
Life can be pondered so pointless when no more is gained
Reflection on mortality can maketh thee wretched
When the needs of the spirit lie yet unsustained

They recall oft death, as the destroyer of pleasures
And throw their bodies like flowers on top of the grave
"Can not thee rise? Can not thee walketh? This cannot be that
    we'll not kiss again!
Please thee to returneth and all promises I give! Please thee to
    returneth and all wrongs is forgave!"

To this end, therefore, you could see that true happiness wilt come,
From connection with the most wondrous fountain of old Lazarus
But be each setteth to be of the time thou hast now
And with graciousness and provision may thou be made rapturous

Returneth thee not dear, to dark Loch Talamah
You'll find no satisfaction, only gloom and despair
Inter thy love in strong coffin and hurry thee hence
For where the departed still pace there is only dead air

Under the soil there is no need to cope with these feelings,
Or pardon yourself to those who doth not understand,
When alone, one thus haunted dost not bethink rightly
Slay your appetency, I pray you, for this wanion'ed land

Search not for your walking and ashen dead lover
Go home you my dear, go home you and weep
Loch Talamah will find you wherever you lie
So go home you to bed now, go home you and sleep

Slow Burn

he was successfully hooked,
in one quick movement,
Mr. Martinez
waited
in
the right frame of mind,
a rhythmic Zen
I
used to search
I was looking for
a cartoon villain

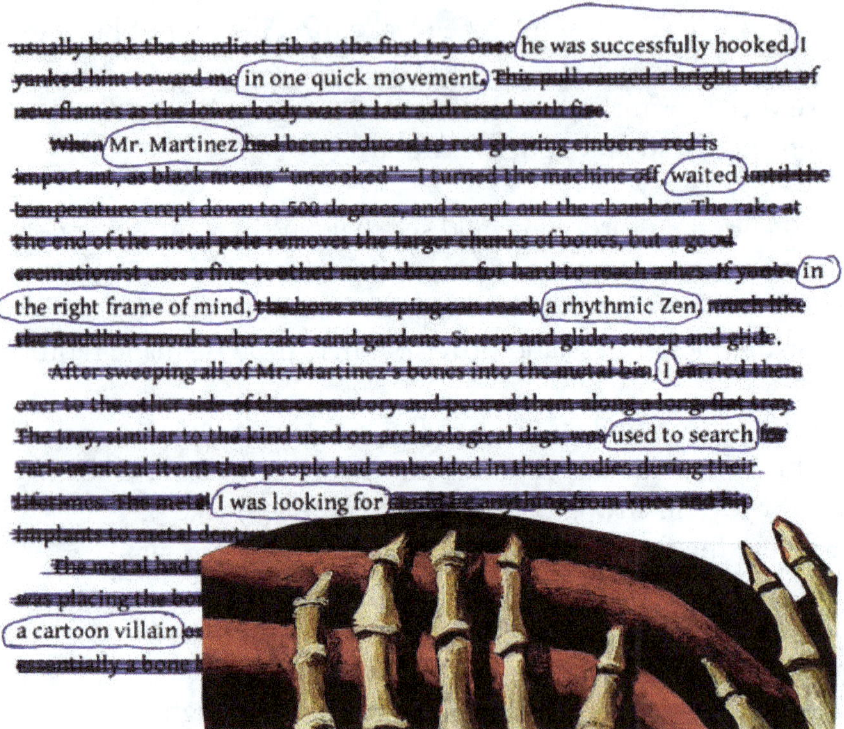

Source: "Smoke Gets in Your Eyes & Other Lessons from the Crematory"
by Caitlin Doughty   [W.W. Norton & Company, 2014]

McLord Selasi

The Carousel of Lost Children

The painted horses rise and fall,
In endless circles, heeding the call
Of music box melodies twisted with age,
While rust eats slowly through their cage.

Empty saddles creak and sway,
Where children once would laugh and play.
Now shadows ride these wooden steeds,
Through carnival grounds gone to weeds.

I've watched them come on autumn nights,
When frost turns moonbeams into knives.
Their small forms flicker as they queue,
To mount the horses, two by two.

They wear the clothes of different eras:
A boy in knickers, girls in mirrors
Of fashion long since laid to rest,
Each phantom child a former guest.

The organ wheezes ancient tunes,
Below the watchful harvest moon.
While brass rings tarnish on their poles,
These children reach for distant goals.

Around and 'round the platform turns,
While somewhere distant, gas light burns.
The carnival barker's endless spiel,
Echoes through this broken wheel.

Some nights I count them as they ride:
The drowning victim, blue inside;
The fever child with vacant stare;
The twins who vanished at the fair.

Their laughter sounds like breaking glass,
As 'round and 'round the horses pass.
Each revolution marks the years
Since they first disappeared in tears.

The mechanism grinds its gears,
Oiled by a century of fears.
While parents still post missing signs,
Their children ride these endless lines.

I've tried to shut the power down,
To still these horses' endless round.
But even with no current flowing,
They keep their midnight circuit going.

The paint peels off in leprous strips,
While time's decay slowly grips
These once-bright steeds of joy and wonder,
Now bearing souls that wander under

The carnival's decaying tent,
Where happiness and horror blent.
Each night they gather, young and fair,
To ride their carousel of despair.

And sometimes when the moon is right,
New children join them in their flight.
Fresh shadows mount the waiting steeds,
To satisfy the carousel's needs.

So if you pass this haunted ground,
Don't pause to listen to the sound
Of tinkling music in the dark,
Or children's laughter in the park.

For once you hear the organ play,
You might be drawn to join their way,
Another rider, young and bold,
Upon these horses growing old.

Jack Granath

The Room

The room is always subterranean.
Your foot projects you from the bottom stair,
And you begin to lurch through half-lit halls,
A maze—no, not exactly—though you are

Unquestionably lost. At last, your fear
Of finding it or not is tipped before
The vision of the dreaded thing you seek,
A pure black block against the dust-brown gloom,

Rectangular, the entrance to the room,
Where you know only that you will be changed,
Emerge as something turned into another,
An empty self, unwilled, a double-goer.

You know you must. You doubt it, but you do.
You move into the nightmare in the nightmare.

Juleigh Howard-Hobson

The Snare

It's not real, you know it isn't real. How
could
that clearing be there, right here, right now.
These woods
aren't where things like that are found.
Buildings do
not spring from forest floors, bound
by trees. If you
are smart, you'll walk on past.
And you won't wonder
why it's appeared, vast
and huge, leaning under
some unreal weight
beneath that canopy of
soft fog. Bait's
always fascinating enough
to make
you think about how much you'd like to
take
it. If you approach that farmhouse, you're through.

C. Payne

The Talking Board

The lights dim, and girls giggle with
    excitement
hallways emptying as they bide their time.
They quietly creep from the safety of warm
    beds
to gather where the headmistress can't see,
the thrill of danger and the forbidden
coursing through their adolescent thoughts;
fearful of the game that will soon begin,
yet too innocent to understand why.

Whispers cease, and eyes grow wide
as they circle around the oracle.
Letters crudely etched into a cutting board
filled with the promise of divination;
a broken pair of eyeglasses
playing the part of planchette,
the words YES, NO, GOODBYE
completing the talking board.

Candles flickering with every breath,
they invite the dead to speak;
preparing the questions they wish to ask,
false bravado in every voice.
They place trembling hands together
lightly touching the spirit board;
the cold grows teeth, and shadows strengthen
as the planchette begins to move.

The game begins—

"Are there any spirits here?"
        YES

no

"Can you join us?"
        F-O-R-E-V-E-R

"Will I ever fall in love?"
        NO

"Am I pretty?"
        Y-O-U A-R-E S-E-E-N

(nervous laughs as a form of release)

"Will we be rich and famous?"
        NO

"Will we live long and happy lives?"
    S-I-C-K Y-O-U W-I-L-L B-E S-I-C-K
        A-N-D S-U-F-F-E-R

(silence)

"When?"
        N-O-W

Convulsions wrap them in arms of pain,
eyes bleeding as young bodies rebel;
the board screaming hate all the while
they retch their steaming insides out.
Together, but alone at the end of life,
they won't be found 'til the morning comes;
unmoving, hands upon the broken board
planchette resting on the word GOODBYE.

Ron Perovich

The Woods

There are places in the world
So old, they're haunted on their own;
Inhabited by ageless malice
Wishing to be left alone.
Long before our first trespass,
When mankind still remained asleep,
It lay cursing in the dark,
For all the company it would keep.

The Bruckners carried to their graves
The weight of grief, for their lone boon,
Their only son of summer days,
Who ran ahead of them, too soon.
A boy of six and as many months
Who loved too much to run and play,
Especially in those twisted woods
Shoeless in the humus and clay.
Darling Eggert, so like the wind,
To fly and swirl between the trunks,
And kick up all the leaves and dust
Until he found beneath it, sunk,
A root just right to wrench small feet
And draw him to the leafy bed,
Where likewise lay an angled rock
To catch his soon well-rested head.

The Yeager brothers feared no bear
When chasing game to run it down.
They were as lean as moonlight rays
Thinly piercing that canopy's crown.
The black stag dodged their every shot
Or seemed to as it led them deep
Into the thick and branching night,
'Til darkly lost, they stopped to sleep.
By rote and touch they built a fire
And laid upon the chilling earth,
Bundled in their flax and wool
To doze amid the smoke and turf.
It's said they dreamt of cooking meat,
When one was woken by the screams
Of his brother, now a candle
From sparks that weren't just in his dreams.

Poor Greta Friedman had her wish
To take on the Baumgartner name,
Via the hand of Mickel the Younger,
A painter who had felt the same.
He courted her by way of portraits
Cast in oils of rose and white,
Insisting on only natural settings
Where he could catch her natural light.
And so he sat her beneath an elm
Near the edge of that wild,
To balance the gloom of the forest behind
With autumn skies and weather mild.
She sat as still as the dead, alas,
Before the paint of her lips had set
A bough above him released with a crack
And saving his work, he delayed, with regret.

Many human lifetimes later
(But not so many for the trees)
The hunger for lumber caught up with the wood
And a company came to take what they please.
Breezes and bees were drowned out by saws
As the crash of giants roared through the vale.
Mighty chains crisscrossed the hillside
To drag or lift; to bind up and bale.
Between working men, the lines threaded up,
Up the steep ground, 'round stump and machine,
Straining taut against hundreds of tons
But there was a flaw that had gone yet unseen.
One link was all it took to break,
And release all that force waist-high from the floor,
To whip the chain through flesh, bone, and leather,
And turn a dozen men into twenty-four.

There are places in the world,
That once were haunted on their own.
Now they're cursing in the wind
All the ghosts who've made it home.

Stephen A. Roddewig

The Traveler

The moon rose into the night,
The woodland creatures shrunk away,
Recoiling, the darkness was slashed by gray light,
Silence fell over the meadow with the dew,
All animals caught in the talons of fright,
The nightmare had begun anew.

Before the full moon, the townsfolk shuddered,
Axes sharpened, rifles loaded,
Doors locked, windows shuttered,
Lanterns smothered, the stillness foreboding,
Prayers for mercy quickly muttered.

Far off, amongst a thicket of pines,
Deep in the rolling, creeping hills,
A gaping maw opened, a long-abandoned mine,
In the air, full of fear and chills,
Gray beams plunged down into the dark recesses,
A howl ripped through the night, the call of the kill.

All heard the ghostly dirge,
Knowing the end was nigh,
The beast had come to purge,
There was nowhere to hide.

Rising, the corpse crawled from the muck,
Flesh and bone growing strong,
Fate had never shown the abomination luck,
For it was dead no longer,
Dull eyes glistened, gray arms shook,
For it began to hunger.

Its eyes sliced far into the gloom, seeking victims,
Snout rooting them out as their fear-scent thickened,
Charging forth, the beast lumbered through the trees,
Vast shoulders, teeth, and claws killing all it sees,
Deer, rabbits, birds, even sheep it ate,
All living creatures were its bait.

Aye, but for one it had gained a taste,
A hunger no woodlander could slate,
The human's flesh, warm in its teeth,
Of this it had a raving need,
Nearing the village, its jaws salivated.

A volley of shot greeted the gruesome visitor,
But black powder and Winchesters only made it move quicker,
Rushing forth, the bravest attacked with shovels and axes,
Death feasted, bodies flying as his claws slashed,
The roar of Satan's minion tore through the glen,
Every mortal knew the bell tolled for them.

Leagues away, upon a trodden woodland road,
A traveler rode, his horse whimpering at the call of wrath,
Picking up the reins, the man galloped down the path,
Along the river stood a church, decrepit and old,
Yes, this would do, as lure and stronghold.

Windows, doors, walls,
All meant nothing as the beast stood tall,
Blood covered its muzzle, bodies littered at its feet,
But years had made it insatiable; the hunt was not complete.

As the iron bell tolled, red eyes turned 'round,
Massive paws pummeled the ground, leaving the ruined town,
Tree trunks, vines, streams, and clearings passed as it ran,
Seeking another victim, this blight of the land,
The enemy of man.

Atop the steeple, the traveler waited,
His horse tethered below, the hook baited,
Thunder charged towards the churchyard,
The man shouldered his rifle, aiming down the sights,
One, two, three conical rounds took flight,
It stumbled; the beast had been scarred!

Slinging his firearm onto his back,
His boots thumped down the stairs,
Instinct and ferocity it didn't lack,
Now was not the time to be careless,
He found it stalking toward his horse,
He answered with fiery discourse.

The shot caught the beast in the head,
But not a drop of blood was shed,
The traveler felt his boots turning to lead,
No creature could survive silver, it was said,
Its paws lashed out in rage, the fencepost broken.

Full of panic, the narrowly spared horse fled,
The traveler leaped as the stallion crashed into him,
Head spinning, he lay on the ground as his nose bled,
Watching as the beast approached with a crimson grin,
It opened its jaws, ready to swallow him whole,
Grabbing his rifle, he smashed it against the skull.

Rolling away from the behemoth,
The traveler scrambled to his feet,
A paw seized the gun; it'd had enough,
He released it, fighting the urge to flee.

There! As it stumbled backwards,
An axe in its side, it revealed,
It swung as the man rushed forward,
Ducking, he tore the pole out with zeal,
Winding back, with fire he yelled,
Striking once! Twice! Until it stilled,
The enemy of man, man had felled.

In the crimson dawn, the trees swayed,
A pair of boots broke the silence,
Amidst the shattered structures, the stillness,
Amongst the legions of the slain,
With the utmost reverence,
A gray, gruesome head was laid,
So the dead would know,
Justice was done that day.

Lance McVay

The Hunger of Horace Leach

Horace Leach
Was the shape of a peach,
With a monocle held by a chain.
He had a thin mustache,
And loads of cash,
And walked with a silver-tipped cane.

He was known to be proud
And ever so loud
And praised by his false-faced friends,
But when push came to shove
He was never so loved
Like the day that he came to his end.

He owned a steamer line
And would wine and dine
His elegant guests on the deck;
Would harangue the crew,
And the captain too,
Right up to the day of the wreck.

No one understood,
The weather was good,
The heading was due true North
No one saw it coming,
But then came the drumming
And it roared with a turbulent force.

A wave like Gibraltar
Caused it to falter;
The ship rolled and tumbled and broke,
And sank like a stone
With bodies and bone
And all of those elegant folk.

But not Horace Leach;
He awoke on a beach,
Covered in seaweed and sand.
With a handful of crew
And some passengers too,
Who offered an outstretched hand.

On that small desert isle
They lived for a while
Off boxes that floated ashore.
And the people and crew
Were fishing too
To stock up the food-stuffs more.

But not Horace Leach,
From day one at the beach
Hadn't lifted a finger or foot.
He hollered and whined
And only would dine
In his hut where he told them to put

Everything they collected,
'Cause he had directed
That anything coming ashore
Was his by the law
And all that they saw
Should be tallied and sorted and stored.

He found a deck chair
Where he'd sit and stare
At the ladies who swam the lagoon.
He'd bloviate and brag
And improperly grab
The ladies and look the buffoon.

At night by the fire,
With everyone tired
Of counting and rationing food,
Old Horace would yell
And proceeded to tell
Every soul of his souring mood.

"I'm hungry, you hear?
So bring bread and beer,
Some crackers and biscuits and cheese.
Make good time
And bring me what's mine;
You'd be starving if it weren't for me."

Weeks came and went
And the rations were spent;
The castaways pale and gaunt.
But not Horace Leach
Who continued to preach
His whining and wailing and wants.

"I've run out of wine.
And we're short on time
For today…we shall run out of meat.
So, I'm ready to ask
An unthinkable task
Of deciding just who we should eat."

"I think we should draw
The proverbial straws,
Then quickly we'll kill, cook and eat
The unfortunate soul
Who will play that role
I think we can do one a week."

Well, three weeks passed,
When finally, at last,
A vessel that was well off-course,
Discovered the crew
And the passengers who,
By the captain, were welcomed aboard.

"Oh, you look well-fed.
How many are dead?"
"Just one," they said, with a sigh.
"But he gave all he had.
It was so very sad;
The day that Horace Leach died."

And so, to this day
Some people will say
On an island you'll find the remains
of Mr. Horace Leach
Not far from the beach
Marked with a silver-tipped cane.

But it's been noted,
If you're so devoted
To finding his place of last rest,
Don't be too shocked
When under that rock
You discover there isn't much left.

Darrell Z. Grizzle

The Visitor

I can always tell when you're coming to visit;
The smell of the makeshift grave precedes you.
I make my way down to the cellar,
to save you the walk up the stairs.
I look at your ruined form,
that once strong body, now rotting away.

Ours was always a forbidden love.
Now, even more so.

You greet me with your attempt at a smile;
The effort means a lot.
I lay my hand on your chest. Your heart is still.

There's just enough left of your face to see your smile,
the one I fell in love with.
There's just enough left of your arms for me to surrender
to your once warm, now cold, embrace.

Lauren Swiderski

𝕻𝖊𝖕 𝖙𝖆𝖑𝖐

It's true
Persephone winters with her confusion
and Orpheus grieves in his cups,
but hear me out:
Not all trips to the underworld are bad.
When you know the sound of summons—it
    quakes the earth
and cracks you open like an egg—
do not despair. Breathe deeply, take heart.
Bring biscuits for Cerberus, a tip for the
    ferryman.
A little kindness makes a good impression, it
    goes a long way
when you've nowhere to go but down,
down in this darkling town, with
charcoal prayers clawed raw on rock-face,
blind open-mouthed blind gargoyles
glaring out from a spindling staircase,
their baby bird tongues reaching, vibrating,
hungry to be heard for their music, sweet and
    yearning.
It scrapes your insides down,
it draws your throat-strings tight but you
    must sing;
Scream, even—you'll not want for the
    difference,
you'll see, finally, how
flying down the steps,
transcending circles of inferno becomes a
    game of hopscotch
Scrub-a-dub-dub yourself down in clean,
    good fire

Throw your shadow on the wall, tall as you
    dare,
Give it fangs and claws
and LAUGH at it,
Find your pettiest demons and invite them all
    to tea
Find Hades himself and take him to bed (not
    the perfect gentleman, but what a lover)
Indeed: think of hell as a holiday!
Isn't it better than wandering through the
    woods midlife
Gray hair growing long and brittle,
the trees prattling where are your children
    come to get you?
Oh, oh,
but it will get darker, my dear
and colder
so, do remember to bring a torch.

Chuck Mckenzie

The Girl With No Eyes

At the urging of my bladder
I shuffle down the hallway,
past the bedrooms of my children,
now empty, touched by dust and rot;
past the aging, wonky bookshelves
that my opa made by hand,
and pau-pau's ancient school desk that
we simply left there and forgot.

And despite it being 2 a.m.
and all about me, darkness,
my step is very certain
having trod this path before.
I, as always, only falter
as I pass the kitchen entrance
and I sense the little dead girl
glaring from beyond the door.

I have felt her since I moved here,
almost thirty years this winter;
felt her rage and felt her loathing
from the day this house was mine.
Early on I wondered whether
I was losing all my marbles,
'til I started seeing movements
from the corner of my eye.

A small and shifting figure
in the darkness near the oven,
never speaking, only glowering,
in the middle of the night.
And the waves of hate and anger
that flow from her keep me looking
anywhere but actually at her,
lest my heart stop at the sight.

Despite living here for decades
and acknowledging the haunting
I have seen her only once now,
just five or six years past,
when one night, too full of merlot
and staggering to the toilet,
I thoughtlessly turned, staring,
and froze in my tracks, aghast.

A small child of maybe eight or nine
dressed in Victorian clothing,
with a long and threadbare nightdress
I could see completely through.
And she stared back with such venom
from dark pits where eyes had once been,
opened up her mouth and, shrieking,
raised her hands and at me flew.

She chased me, stumbling, screaming,
all the way back up the hallway,
crashing from one piece of furniture
to the next along the wall.
She caught me at my bedroom.
I had slammed the door behind me,
Yet, I felt an ice-cold finger
brush my back, and then I fell.

Pain exploded in my chest
as numbness tingled both my arms.
Heart attack, I thought, and dialled
for the ambos right away.
I felt her staring from the darkness
of the kitchen as they took me
to the hospital that night
for an almost week-long stay.

Rushed to surgery, they saved me.
Such a close thing, they opined,
though they couldn't understand what
blocked my artery that day.
When I finally returned
to my dark and brooding home
I could sense her savage glee
at having nearly got her way.

Since then, my sight has worsened,
and if I do not turn my head
I no longer see her moving
in my periphery.
But despite feeling her hate still
burning in the darkened kitchen,
my fear has diminished into a
sense of inevitability.

I am tired all the time now,
always weary to the bone.
And pain is a constant presence,
like that of my vengeful foe.
Is that twinge inside my breast
from where they inserted the stent?
Every chest pain leaves me wondering
Is this a cardiac event?

And I know that one day soonish,
whether from a dicky ticker
or from making full eye contact
with that ghostly little girl,
or for far more mundane reasons,
someone knocking at the front door
(perhaps looking through the mail slot)
will see me lying where I fell.

And I honestly and truly
hope that there'll be nothing after.
Just to be gone would be preferable
to the bleak alternative:
to be trapped right here forever
in my house, alone but for that
single unforgiving spectre
who will haunt me, evermore.

So let death be a release
and let the darkness bring me peace.
If I'm offered up a preference
then I'd truly rather die
than to walk these rooms eternally,
ever fearful of the presence
of that grim Victorian phantom—
The Girl With No Eyes.

Joshua Dobson

What Waits Behind the Tiny Black Door

In the shadow-shrouded attic
of a burnt house,
I discovered a tiny black door,
like one might find
in a child's playhouse.
From behind the black door
crept a sickeningly sweet smell
(nauseatingly pungent
even to a nose deadened
by two floors of smoke,
soot, and wet ashes)
and a faint rhythmic wheezing noise,
like the snoring
of an emphysema patient
echoing down a long hallway.
Why am I opening the door?
I asked myself
as my luminously pale hand
undid the rusty latch.
As the tiny black door creaked open
and the jaundiced moonlight
that oozed through
the holes in the roof
fell upon that which waited behind it,
I was surprised.
I always thought it would be bigger.
Then it opened.

About the Authors & Artists

AJ Bartholomew – Amber Eyes

AJ Bartholomew is a writer and poet from Northern Virginia who enjoys a good horror story. AJ would like to publish a book of horror limericks one day.

Akis Linardos – When You Space Out, I Take Control

Akis is a writer of oddities, a researcher, and maybe human. Read him in *Apex*, *Uncharted*, *Strange Horizons*, and more at linktr.ee/akislinardos.

Alex Carrigan – Wicked Stepmother Golden Shovel

Alex Carrigan (he/him) is a Pushcart-nominated editor, poet, and critic from Alexandria, VA. He is the author of *Now Let's Get Brunch* and *May All Our Pain Be Champagne*. carriganak.wordpress.com

Alex Fine – Parasite

Alex is a seventeen-year-old nonbinary artist from South Africa, in love with the dark, the weird, and obscure.

Amanda M. Blake – Sins of the Asylum

A mass of tentacles and rose vines masquerading as a person, Amanda is the author of such titles as *Question Not My Salt*, *Deep Down*, and *Out of Curiosity and Hunger*. amandamblake.com

Anna Kirby – Faith, hope, and charity

Anna Kirby's collages are sensory poems that express the complex emotions surrounding PTSD, abuse, child loss, infertility, and female identity, made using secondhand books, scissors, glue dots, and oil paints. www.annakirby.com

Anna McCluskey – Drip

Anna McCluskey is an Oregon–based, almost–entirely–feral fantasy author. In addition to her books, she's had several poems published, and her short fiction has been read by at least a dozen people, many of whom murmured appreciatively about it. annamccluskey.com

Anne Anthony – Death Lurks in the Walls

Anne Anthony's digital collages have been published in literary journals including *Ghost Parachute, Remington Review*, and *Mom Egg Review*. See more of her art: anneanthony.weebly.com/portfolio1.html

AriBo – Nevermore

Arianna "Aribo" Bosa – illustrator, graphic designer, badass sweetheart. Based in Italy. Draws anatomy, explores decaying beauty, and creates from emotion, obsession, and spite. Instagram/Threads @ariboart

Azure Arther – A Gorgon at the End of the World

When she's not a harpy bodyguard for her very own little prince, Azure Arther is a multi–disciplinary artist, professor and editor. Find her at azurearther.com.

Bernardo Villela – In the Distance Dark (Gargoyle Poem #1)

Bernardo Villela lives in Wilmington, Delaware. He has short fiction included in periodicals such as *LatineLit* and *Horror Tree*. He's had poetry published by Phantom Kangaroo, Straylight, and Raven's Quoth Press. linktr.ee/bernardovillela

Blayne Waterloo – LEASHED

Blayne Waterloo (they/she) is a horror writer and editor living in Georgia with their partner and loud pets. Find their work at ewhag.com

Brandon Case – Nightmare Narcosis

Brandon Case is a golden retriever who writes of unsettling worlds. He has recent work in *Escape Pod*, *Flash Fiction Online*, and *Small Wonders*, among others. Twitter, Instagram @BrandonCase101 | brandoncase. net

C. Payne – The Talking Board

C. Payne claims to be born in a cemetery, under the sign of the moon. His work has appeared in Witch House Magazine, Just Keep Up, and other various anthologies and publications.

Callum Wilson – Layered House

Callum Wilson is an MFA in Writing graduate from the University of Saskatchewan and Miscellaneous Editor at BTWN Magazine. He lives in Canada where he makes weird music, writes weird things, and takes photos of bugs.

Camellia Paul – Date Night

Camellia Paul is a graduate student of Comparative and World Literature at the University of Illinois at Urbana–Champaign. Her poetry, translation, and art regularly appear in magazines and anthologies.

Caterina Minezzi – The Abyss

Born in a small town near Bologna, Caterina Minezzi has had a love for the bizarre and the macabre since she was a child. Rebirth, the desire to change, and emotions are all recurring themes in her art. Instagram @ cat.min.art

Christopher Collingwood – Playing Fetch with the Demon Boar

Chris was born and raised in Sydney Australia. Chris has devoted his spare time to writing, with works published in *Not One of Us*, *Andromeda Spaceways*, and other dimensionally unstable places.

Chuck Mckenzie – The Girl With No Eyes
Chuck McKenzie is an award–nominated author of SF and horror fiction. daftnotions.com/chuck–mckenzie

Claudia Tong – The Winter of Our Discontent
Claudia Tong is multidisciplinary artist based in London, creating at the intersection of physical and digital art. With a background in computer science and quantitative finance, she has lived, studied, worked and exhibited internationally. linktr.ee/claudiaxt

Corinne Pollard – See Here
Corinne Pollard is a disabled UK horror writer and poet, published multiple times such as with Black Hare Press, A Coup of Owls, and Carnage House Publishing. corinnepollard.wordpress.com

Daniel Barlekamp – There's a Coffin in My Parlor!
Daniel Gene Barlekamp is the author of poetry, fiction, and audio drama for adults and young readers. He lives with his family in Massachusetts. dgbarlekamp.com

Darrell Z. Grizzle – The Visitor
Darrell Z. Grizzle is a poet and writer of horror, dark fantasy, and crime fiction. His home on the web is ShadowHaunted.com.

David Bennett Black – Foraging for Fruit: A Coward's Poem
David Bennett Black is a rapscallion. With various shorts being published in a number of different anthologies in the next twelve months, he truly believes that people may actually start enjoying his company now.

Dee Allen. – Mirielle
African-Italian performance poet based in Oakland, California. Author of 10 books and 81 anthology appearances.

Delana Luna – Cabin Fever

Delana Luna is a spirit-led artist that uses all her subtle channels to walk between worlds, traverse the collective unconscious and ancestral lines to bring back stories of myth, magic and alternate dimensions. themuseumofmagicalobjects.com

Drew Golden – Storm Light

Drew Golden is an author and artist from Pennsylvania and writes under the pen name D.K. Golden. His short stories have appeared in speculative fiction magazines and his novel, *Nightingale*, is available from Dorrance Publishing

Edward Lodi – Meet the Monsters

Edward Lodi writes, eats, sleeps, and performs other bodily functions in Hingham, Massachusetts.

Em Arata-Berkel – Is Something Wrong

Em Arata-Berkel is an emerging poet who's taken root in the Pacific Northwest. They earn coin by untangling taxonomies and are seldom without a cup of coffee. Their poetry can be found in the award-winning anthology *I Sing the Salmon Home: Poems from Washington State.* erratawrites.bsky.social

Eryn Hiscock – After Frankenstein

Eryn lives in Toronto. She's nearing completion of her first speculative/science fiction novel.

Evan Baughfman – 3 SPOOKY Haikus

Evan Baughfman is the author of *Vanishing of The 7th Grade, Bad for Your Teeth, Try Not to Die in a Dark Fairy Tale,* and *Mauls of the Wild.*

Foong – In The Stillness

Foong writes for a living and draws to manage her stress. She creates worlds and new realms through both forms of art. linktr.ee/phoenixfoong

Gary Every – Necropoliti

Gary Every is an award-journalist and well published science fiction author. He has two published novellas available *Inca Butterflies* and *The Saint and the Robot*.

Glenis Moore – Fright Night

Glenis Moore currently lives in the flat lands of the Fens, UK and her poetry can be viewed on her SubStack page at glenis15.substack.com

Greg Beatty – When I die, I will walk

Greg Beatty lives in Bellingham, Washington. He writes everything from jokes about cows to essays on cooking disasters, and has more dog friends than human friends. greg-beatty.com

Greg Schwartz – Vessel

Greg Schwartz has been a copier repairman, fitness instructor, and bartender, with varying degrees of success. His poems have appeared in *Talebones*, *Rattle*, and *Asimov's*.

Gregg Chamberlain – The Zombie Came Back

Gregg Chamberlain lives in rural Ontario, Canada, with his missus, Anne, and their cats, who use zombies as scratching posts. facebook.com/gregg.chamberlain

Gregory M Thompson – The Lighthouse Keeper

Gregory M. Thompson is a horror, science fiction, and fantasy writer with a variety of credits in online and print magazines and anthologies. He lives in Illinois with his wife, son, and troublemaking Chocolate Lab. nightcrynovel.com

Hailey Samford – Literal

Hailey Samford is from Texas, working in the early morning as an HVAC dispatcher while dealing with cats, story writing, and the wild weather.

Hannah Rebekah Graves – Masters of Horror

Hannah is the thing that lives under the sink. She will sometimes appear if left offerings of moss and teeth. creepshannah.com

Hannan Khan – Eternity

Hannan Khan — a nefelibata, poet & scholar of literature & linguistics from Pakistan. He sips coffee & reads Manto. For a glimpse into his life, find him on Instagram: @hannan.khan.official

Henna Oak – Homage

Henna Oak (she, her) is a college student in St. Paul, Minnesota where she is majoring in creative writing and geology. In her free time she enjoys saving spiders, learning Icelandic, and watching horror movies with her mother.

Henry Corrigan – you and yours are Mine

Henry Corrigan is a bisexual poet, and the award-winning author of *A Man In Pieces* (Bloodhound Books) and *Somewhere Quiet, Full of Light* (Slashic Horror Press). Follow him on Instagram: Instagram @ henrycorrigan08

Ian Bain – I Am a Human Nesting Doll

Ian A. Bain is a writer of dark fiction from the swamps of Ontario. He can be stalked online at @bainwrites on Instagram, Bluesky, or Threads.

Ian Klink – Rain, Rain, Go Away...

As a filmmaker, writer, and artist, Ian Klink's work includes the feature film *Anybody's Blues*, the novel *Lucky* (New Fangle Press), and short stories and poetry for a number of anthologies.

J. Agombar – Trail Gone Cold

J. Agombar resides near the treacherous waters of Southend-On-Sea, Essex, UK where visions of the speculative, criminal, and supernatural have taken over his mind (usually alongside a bottle of whisky).

J. E. Norwood – Laughter After Dark

J. E. Norwood lives amidst the mists of Scotland. When he's managed to rip himself away from the writing chair (or let's be honest, couch), he's either gardening, reading or bouldering.

J. J. Munro – Idi Amin's Brain

J. J. Munro is an Australian who writes noir and horror fiction as J. J. Munro. His work has appeared via Akashic Books, Black Hare Press, and now Graveside Press!

J. Weintraub – Halloweens Past

J. Weintraub's publications include fiction, essays, poetry, and translations along with over 50 productions of his dramatic work in the USA and internationally. jweintraub.weebly.com

Jack Granath – The Room

Jack Granath is a librarian in Kansas. jackgranath.com

Jacqueline K Goldblatt – Before He Stays

Jacqueline K. Goldblatt is an NJ–based writer whose works are often moody, dark, and unafraid to embrace the weird. When not hunched over a laptop you can find her playing TTRPGS with her friends and taking walks at unreasonable hours of the night. jackiefrostling.carrd.co

Jayde Fontana – The Prying Eye

Jayde Fontana (they/she) is a poet, short-story writer, and aspiring novelist. As a non-binary transgender woman, Jayde aims to bring diversity and inclusion to all of her work. Instagram @jayde_fontana_writing

JB Wocoski – When the Black Cat Mews

JB Wocoski retired in 2015, he now has fun writing poetry and stories for online magazines and anthologies. His self-published books are available on Amazon. facebook.com/profile.php?id=61556353635813

Jeff L Oliver – Apocalyptic Sun

Jeff Oliver was born in Baltimore, Maryland on April 6th, 1982. A poet by passion and father of eight beautiful children, his dedication to his family and his craft is intense. joliver3334.substack.com

Jim G. Burns – snapshots from the hole

Jim Burns was born and raised in rural Indiana and spent most of his working life as a librarian. In retirement he turned to writing. He lives with his wife and dog in Jacksonville, Florida.

JJ Carpenter – I Am Haunted

Award–winning author JJ Carpenter is an Australian poet and novelist fascinated with dark history, the macabre, and human connections. jjcarpenterauthor.com

John Grey – A Winter of the Soul

John Grey is an Australian poet, US resident, recently published in *New World Writing*, *River And South* and *The Alembic*. Latest books, *Bittersweet*, *Subject Matters* and *Between Two Fires* are available now. themindfulword. org/poems–grey–uffizi

Jonathan Ukah – My Father Dies a Second Time

Jonathan Chibuike Ukah is a Nigerian-born poet living in the United Kingdom. His poems have been featured in literary magazines and anthologies.

Joshua Dobson – a slug in the eye, What Waits Behind the Tiny Door

Joshua Dobson invented the theory of (but not yet recipe for) the Lemon–Vanilla Marinade, a tricky blend of acid and base which, if ever achieved in actuality will redefine flavor.

Juleigh Howard-Hobson – The Snare

Juleigh Howard–Hobson's poetry has appeared in *Amazing Stories*, *The Dead Lands*, *Audient Void*, *Under Her Skin* (Black Spot) *Vastarien: Women's Horror* (Grimscribe), and other places. X @PoetForest

Julia LaFond – Wolves
Julia LaFond has a master's in geoscience and writes SFF/H fiction and poetry when she's not playing or running games. jklafondwriter.wordpress.com

Julius – Reflection
Julius (they/them) is a nonbinary artist from the Northwest Coast of California.

Katherine Garrison – Castle Reflections
Katherine Garrison writes short fiction and poetry exploring themes through the lens of nature, food, the weird, or some mix of these. katherinegarrison.bsky.social

Katherine Kerestman – Bobby's Adventure
Katherine Kerestman is the author of *Lethal* (Psychotoxin Press, 2023), *Creepy Cat's Macabre Travels: Prowling around Haunted Towers*, and others. Her name is etched among the inscrutable glyphs of the Esoteric Order of Dagon and the Dracula Society. creepycatlair.com

Katherine Quevedo – Peter Pumpkin Eater's Most Delectable Carving
Katherine Quevedo is an analyst and writer from Portland, Oregon. Her speculative poems and stories have been nominated for the Pushcart, Rhysling, and Elgin awards. katherinequevedo.com

Kelli Dianne Rule – If
Kelli Dianne Rule is an three–time art school dropout and author of dark fiction who claims roots in the backwoods of Florida. Follow her work at kellirule.com and kdiannerule@bsky.social

Kenneth Donald Reimer – The Song of the Corpse
Kenneth D. Reimer lives on the Canadian Great Plains with his wife, Lisa, and a cat named Nazca who likes to bite him on the leg. kennethdreimer.com

Kevin Anderson – Nightmare

Kevin David Anderson, writes sci-fi/horror novels, short stories, and even joke books. His latest book is *Try Not To Die in Roswell.* KevinDavidAnderson.com

Klaus Iliff Hageman – The "Ballad" of Talamah Loch

When Klaus was only two MTV introduced them to their first experience with horror, Michael Jackson's Thriller. Years later, they embraced the opportunity to write their own narrative. This set them on the path of horror and Gothic Romanticism, which they continue to indulge in to this day. Threads/Instagram @nix_eradicatus

Krys S Achrem – Please Give Me Scissors

Krys Achrem is a transmasculine agender poet from Las Vegas, Nevada. He was crowned 2022 King of Spades in the Imperial Royal Sovereign Court of the Desert Empire. His hobbies include singing, drawing, and narrating scary stories on Twitch.

Kurt Newton – A Cold, Windswept Place

Kurt Newton's fiction and poetry have appeared in numerous magazines. His fiction collection, *Bruises,* was recently published by Lycan Valley Press. A collection of dark poetry, *Songs of the Underland,* was published by Ravens Quoth Press in 2022. @kurtnewton.bsky. social

Kyle Nowak – Jaded Lament

Kyle Nowak writes weird fiction inspired by Thomas Ligotti and Jon Padgett. He lives in Stevens Point, Wisconsin with his wife and twin daughters...and also his adorable pet leeches. youtube.com/@ TheRenaissancePunk

L.G. Testa – Paradox

Feeling that post-Soviet society did not ensure her enough freedom to express herself in words, L.G. Testa took an interest in the English language. Instagram @laima_27treecrowns

Lance E McVay – The Hunger of Horace Leach

Lance McVay was born in Santa Cruz, California. He now lives in the East Bay Area in Northern California with his wife and twin boys. He teaches and loves to write and tell his ghostly tales of terror and treachery with others when the opportunity arises.

Lauren Swiderski – Pep Talk

Lauren is a writer and artist living in the Pacific Northwest. She draws inspiration from nature, folklore & mythology, and snippets of commentary and conversation. She loves cats, pierogi, and playing the viola da gamba. Her work has recently appeared in *Penumbra Online* and *Locust Shells Journal.* Instagram @laurenswiderski

Lee Clark Zumpe – Poor Little Fellow

Lee Clark Zumpe, an entertainment editor with *Tampa Bay Newspapers,* earned his degree in English at the University of South Florida. Recent publication credits include *Space & Time, Lovecraftiana, Illumen,* and *The Literary Hatchet.* Lee lives on the west coast of Florida with his wife and daughter. @themadpoet.bsky.social

Lillian Csernica – Evil Sirens Sweetly Singing

Lillian Csernica's fiction has appeared in *Weird Tales, Fantastic Stories,* and *Citadels of Darkover.* Fans of steampunk will enjoy her *Kyoto Steampunk* short stories. Born in San Diego, Lillian is a genuine California native. She currently resides in the Santa Cruz mountains with her husband, two sons, and three cats. lillian888.wordpress.com

Lily Black – The Claim

Lily Black is a Polish writer. Her work has appeared in *Sci Phi Journal*, *Flash Point SF* (co–winner of the 2024 Drabble Contest), and *A Coup of Owls*.

Linda M. Crate – & they would die

Linda M. Crate (she/her) is a Pennsylvanian writer who has fifteen published chapbooks, the latest being: *not your piñata* (Alien Buddha Publishing, June 2025). authorlindamcrateswritingnews.blogspot.com

LindaAnn LoSchiavo – My Dungeon Ghost, Slow Burn (Erasure)

Native New Yorker. Poet. Writer. Dramatist. In 2024 *LindaAnn LoSchiavo* had three poetry books published; two titles won multiple awards. Next: *Cancer Courts My Mother* and *Vampire Verses*. vampireventurespoems.com

LL Garland – The Fiddler

LL Garland lives in an old house with three dogs and two haunted libraries. You can find more of her stories at llgarland.com

Lorraine Schein – Ghosts Haunt Space

Lorraine Schein has published in *Strange Horizons*, *Scientific American*, *Star*Line*, and the anthologies *Wild Women* and *Tragedy Queens*. Her latest book is *The Lady Anarchist Cafe*, available from Autonomedia.

M. Brandon Robbins – Heart. Ache.

M. Brandon Robbins is a writer and librarian from Goldsboro, NC. His novel, *Mr. Haunt*, is forthcoming from Sley House Publishing in 2028. mbrandonrobbins.substack.com

Mark Tulin – The Rest Stop

Mark Tulin is a retired therapist from California. He has authored six books and appeared in magazines and anthologies. crowonthewire.com

Matt Dennison – Occasion

Matt Dennison is the author of *Kind Surgery* from Urtica Press (Fr.) and *Waiting for Better* from Main Street Rag Press. His poetry has appeared in *Verse Daily, Rattle, Bayou Magazine, Redivider* and *Cider Press Review*, among others. facebook.com/profile.php?id=100008709036240

McLord Selasi – The Carousel of Lost Children

McLord Selasi is a Ghanaian writer and poet whose work explores memory, identity, and the uncanny. His writing appears in *Eunoia Review* and *Poetry Journal*.

Megan Cartwright – Curios, Post-Op

Megan Cartwright (she/her) is an Australian author and Literature teacher. Her poetry has featured in publications including *Contemporary Verse 2, Cordite Poetry Review* and *Island Magazine*. She is the 2024 recipient of Deakin University's Matthew Rocca Poetry Prize. screechavitch.wixsite.com/mysite

Miranda Allen – Bones Beneath

Miranda Allen is an author and artist living on the north coast of California with her partner, children, and pets.

Murray Eiland – Broken Window

Murray Eiland is a speculative fiction enthusiast. He has a Facebook page "Science Fiction Eiland".

Nancy Byrne Iannucci – Brother

Nancy Byrne Iannucci lives in Troy, NY with her two cats. She is the author of four chapbooks, *Temptation of Wood, Goblin Fruit*, and *Primitive Prayer, Hummingbirds and Cigarettes*. Visit her at nancybyrneiannucci.com Instagram @nancybyrneiannucci

Natalia Díaz Jiménez – Devious Dining

Natalia Díaz Jiménez is a Colombian illustrator, animator and hobbyist photographer, passionate about storytelling and creating immersive worlds through images. natdiazj.wixsite.com/portafolio

Nick Dunkenstein – Guard Your Heart

Nick Dunkenstein, artist by nature and enigma by design. She enjoys long strolls in cemeteries and looking for the dead.

Nicole Field – The Coming of Persephone

Nicole has been writing since they were handed a floppy disc and told how many Word documents could fit on it. They write across the spectrum of sexuality and gender identity in multiple genres. nicolefieldwrites.wordpress.com | faerywhimsy.bsky.social

Odin Meadows – Shuck

Odin Meadows is a horror author and poet living in the Midwest with his husband and two dogs, not too far from the rural town where he grew up. odinmeadows.com

Phillip E. Dixon – Oh, toes

Phillip E. Dixon is an English Professor from Las Vegas who holds an MFA in Writing, puts pineapple on his pizza, and watches too much anime with his cats. philldixon.com

Phinn Disario – What Echoes Are Left

Phinn Disario is a poet and non-fiction writer from New England. His work spans themes of nature's symbolism, visceral horror, and occasionally, spicy dark romance. Find him on Instagram @kophinn.

Red Wallflower – Silence

Meg Wright (Red Wallflower) is a Ditmar Award-winning artistic photographer living in Adelaide, Australia. She's photographed and designed album covers, horror and punk book covers/illustrations, and created a music video. Being neurodivergent and chronically ill, she almost exclusively uses continuous lighting in her work.

Rich McFarlin – I'm sorry, my dear

Rich McFarlin's dearth of life experiences dictate the poetry that springs forth from him and covers any number of topics, including love, heartbreaks and even things that tend to terrify both reader and writer himself.

Ritiksha Sharma – Specimen 401 (a)

Ritiksha is a person. She enjoys scribbling and doodling. Her work has appeared in The *Collidescope, Penumbric Speculative Fiction Magazine* and *Illustrated Worlds Magazine*. X @ritzisharmaa

Rob MacWolf – This Poem Is Haunted

Rob MacWolf lives somewhere in North America waiting for the world to end. In the meantime he writes to keep the fire lit. His first novel, *You Look Lost, Pup*, is available from Bewere Books. You can also find his work in anthologies from the *Furry Historical Fiction Society* and on the audiofiction podcast *The Voice of Dog*. linktr.ee/robmacwolf

Robin Rose Graves – A Reminder

Robin Rose Graves has appeared in *100 Foot Crow, Dark Matter Magazine* and *Simultaneous Times* Podcast. Her debut comes out in 2025 from Graveside Press. Threads @the.book.wormhole

Ron Perovich – The Woods

Artist, musician, and poet Ron Perovich is driven to creative madness by his love of science, history, and scary trees. campsite.bio/ronperovich

Ron Schroer – Hammer Horror

Ron Schroer lives and writes in Canberra, Australia. He writes weird tales based loosely on the weird reality of his surroundings. Visit him at strangefolly.com

Sam Muller – I think I saw you

Sam Muller loves dogs and books. The dogs in her life (currently four) vandalise books. The dogs in her stories solve mysteries and save worlds. sammullerx.substack.com

Sarah E Das Gupta – The Day of the Dead

Sarah Das Gupta is a writer from Cambridge UK. She began writing in 2022 after an accident which has permanently restricted her walking to a few metres. Her work, poetry, flash fiction, short stories, non-fiction and formal essays, has been published in over twenty countries from New Zealand to Kazakhstan.

Stephanie Valente – When We Were Vampires

Stephanie Valente is a poet, copywriter, and the author of the collection *Internet Girlfriend*, published by Clash Books. She is at work on a novel. She lives in Brooklyn, New York. stephanievalente.com

Stephen A. Roddewig – The Traveler

Stephen A. Roddewig is an author from Arlington, Virginia. He is a Horror Writers Association member and has been featured on the *NoSleep* Podcast. stephenaroddewig.com

Stephen Mcquiggan – Invulation

Stephen McQuiggan was the original author of the bible; he vowed never to write again after the publishers removed the dinosaurs and the spectacular alien abduction ending from the final edit. His other, lesser known, novels are *A Pig's View of Heaven* and *Trip a Dwarf*.

Steve Denehan & Robin Denehan – Man, The Empty Room

Steve Denehan lives in Kildare, Ireland with his wife Eimear and daughter Robin. He is the award–winning author of seven poetry collections. stevedenehanpoetry.com

Tehnuka – The New Children

Tehnuka calls on all of us to refuse and resist the genocide of Palestinian people and the colonisation of Palestine. tehnuka.dreamhosters.com

Terry Campbell – The Crow, The Seer

Excessive midnight viewings of American Gladiators helped spawn Terry Campbell's darkly humorous 90s reimagining of Poe's classic *The Raven*. Check out his other works at alittlewestofweird.com

Thomas Sudell – The Bretwalda

Thomas Sudell is a graduate of Oxford University (2015) where he studied English with a speciality in Old English (Anglo-Saxon). Now primarily a translator of ancient poetry both in Old English and Latin, Thomas' main interests are narrative poetry and Gothicism.

Tinamarie Cox – Among the Dead, Feeding the Shadows

Tinamarie Cox flexes her creative abilities through poetry, prose, and art in whatever way she's called. Explore her work at: tinamariethinkstoomuch.weebly.com

Todd Matson – The Feeder

Todd Matson is a Licensed Marriage and Family Therapist. His poetry has been published in *Feminine Collective*, *San Antonio Review* and *The Brussels Review*.

Trace McLaurin – Aren't You Hungry?

Trace McLaurin is a writer and game developer with a passion for finding beauty in the peculiar and the forgotten. Her work strives to be unusual, captivating, and inviting. tracemclaurin.com

Tytti Heikkinen – Come Open the Door

Tytti Heikkinen is a Finnish poet and artist. Her works have appeared in *Amsterdam Review, Ana, Ex–Puritan, Siècle 21 Littérature & Société, Acumen,* and *Offing,* among others.

Vincenzo Cohen – The man and the skull, The Skull

Vincenzo Cohen is an Italian socially engaged multidisciplinary artist. His artistic research is addressed to the representation of social issues such as human rights, and social resilience. vincenzocohen.com

William Shaw – When Shall We Three Meet Again?

William Shaw's writing has appeared in *Strange Horizons, Daily Science Fiction,* and *The Georgia Review.* williamshawwriter.wordpress.com | williamshaw.bsky.social

Yelena Crane – Meat in the Machine

Yelena Crane writes between worlds. Her work explores power that connects, corrupts, and bears consequence. Follow her at @yelenacrane.bsky.social and yelenacrane.com

Reprint Information

A Cold, Windswept Place – Kurt Newton
Tales of Horror, December 2024

After Frankenstein – Eryn Hiscock
The Nashwaak Review, vol. 28/29, 2013 | *Tamaracks: Canadian Poetry for the 20th Century*, 2018

I Think I Saw You – Hailey Samford
The Pedestal Magazine, March 2017

My Dungeon Ghost - LindaAnn LoSchiavo
Women Who Were Warned (Cerasus Poetry), May 2022

Peter Pumpkin Eater's Most Delectable Carving – Katherine Quevedo
HWA Poetry Showcase Vol. XI, October 2024.

The Feeder – Todd Matson
Fright, January 2025

The New Children – Tehnuka
Bloodless (Sliced Up Press), October 2022

The Traveler – Stephen A. Roddewig
ArtAscent Magazine, December 2016

This Poem is Haunted - Rob MacWolf
The Voice of Dog podcast, October 2021

Vessel – Greg Schwartz
Trembles, Nov.–Dec. 2011

When You Space Out, I Take Control – Akis Linardos
Hungry Shadows, 2023

Thank You!

Thank you for supporting Graveside Press and our authors.
One of the biggest ways you can help is to leave a star rating or a
review wherever you purchased your copy!

Stay spooky.

graveside-press.com